MARION JUNIOR HIGH LIBRARY
Two Patriot Drive
Marion, AR 72364

COPING
WHEN

A Parent
Is in Jail

John J. La Valle, D.C.S.W.

THE ROSEN PUBLISHING GROUP, INC./NEW YORK

Published in 1995 by The Rosen Publishing Group, Inc.
29 East 21st Street, New York, NY 10010

Copyright 1995 by John J. La Valle, D.C.S.W.

All rights reserved. No part of this book may be reproduced in any form without permission in writing from the publisher, except by a reviewer.

First Edition

Manufactured in the United States of America

Library of Congress Cataloging-in-Publication Data

La Valle, John J.
    Coping when a parent is in jail / John J. La Valle. —1st ed.
       p.   cm.
    Includes bibliographical references and index.
    ISBN 0-8239-1967-6
    1. Children of prisoners—United States—Juvenile literature.
2. Prisoners—United States—Family relationships—Juvenile literature. 3. Prisons—United States—Juvenile literature.
I. Title.
HV8886.U5L3 1994
362.7—dc20
                                                         94-8245
                                                             CIP

To my father, Joseph G. La Valle, the first person in my life who taught me how to cope with life's adversities.

ABOUT THE AUTHOR ◇

John J. La Valle is a clinical supervisor in the Mental Health Department of Montefiore Medical Center, Rikers Island Health Services. He has also served for two years as a therapist and coordinator of the Crisis Service at Schneider Children's Hospital of the Long Island Jewish Medical Center and has served as a Field Instructor for various schools of Social Work in the New York Area. He maintains a part-time psychoanalytic practice in New York City, in which he works with individuals, families, and groups and provides individual clinical supervision.

Mr. La Valle holds a master's degree in Social Work from New York University and is currently a PhD candidate in Clinical Social Work at that university. In 1989 he received certification in Psychoanalytic Psychotherapy from the Washington Square Institute for Psychoanalytic Psychotherapy and Mental Health.

Contents

1	Shawn's Need to Know	1
2	What Happens on the Inside?	13
3	Visiting	24
4	Women Go to Jail Too	38
5	What Will Happen in Court?	50
6	Prison	61
7	Life after Jail: Parole	72
8	What Does All This Mean about Me?	83
9	Why Do I Need Therapy?	95
10	How to Ask for Help	104
	Appendix	111
	Glossary	113
	For Further Reading	115
	Index	117

CHAPTER ◇ 1

Shawn's Need to Know

Shawn arrived home late, to find his mother and grandmother very upset. They seemed to have been crying. At first he thought they were angry with him. That was his usual first thought: It must be his fault somehow. His conscience began to bother him, and he thought about things he had done wrong. Like most teenagers, he had trouble realizing that sometimes family problems had nothing to do with him. Often they were things he had no control over.

But now he began to see that something else was wrong. His father wasn't home, and he figured that must have something to do with it. When he asked where Dad was, his mother turned away and his grandmother told him not to worry, that everything was okay. That didn't answer his question, and he knew it wasn't true. Anyone could see that something was very wrong. Shawn hated it when they tried to protect him by keeping important information from him. After all, he was fifteen and understood more than they realized. They always encouraged him to come to them when he had problems; why didn't the same rules apply to them? Lacking any information, he could only imagine the worst.

Shawn remembered recent arguments between his parents and thought his father might have left home. Then he wondered whether his father had been hurt. Did he have another fight that landed him in the hospital? Was he in a car accident, or worse, was he dead? What could be so terrible that they had to keep it from him?

Finally Shawn heard his mother talking on the phone and learned that his father had been arrested and was being held in the county jail. He was shocked, but at the same time relieved. And now he had even more questions he was afraid to ask.

Shawn worried about what might happen to his father in jail. Would they hurt him? Then he began to worry about himself and his family. What would happen to them without Dad around to take care of things. Although Shawn always claimed to be old enough to take care of himself, he didn't really believe that. When it came down to it, he needed his father now more than ever.

He avoided asking questions of his mother; he had learned from experience that questions upset her. He couldn't ask someone else because they might not know that his father was in jail, and he didn't want anyone else to know just yet. He was afraid people might make fun of him, or think that his father was bad. If they thought that about his father, what would they think of him or his family.

What made matters even worse was that he felt guilty about his thoughts. How could he let anyone know that he was worried about himself when he was supposed to be worrying about Dad. At the same time, he was angry at his father for disappointing him.

He wondered what Dad had done wrong. He also wondered what it might mean about him; everyone said he was so much like his father. With so many questions on his mind, Shawn began having trouble sleeping at night and concentrating in school. At times he couldn't remember what the teacher had said five minutes after she spoke. He became fidgety and restless and he couldn't keep his mind from wandering. His whole world seemed upside down. He needed someone to talk with.

SHAWN IS NOT ALONE

There are more than a million children like Shawn in the United States. More people than ever before are being arrested and ending up in jail or prison. As the national economy struggles to recover and drug abuse increases, the problem only seems to grow.

According to *USA Today* (February 12, 1992), "If medals were awarded to nations with the most prison inmates, the USA would get the gold." The prison system overflows with 1.1 million inmates, 455 per 100,000 people.

Only the Union of South Africa comes close, and even that racially torn country has experienced a 6.6 percent decrease in prison population, whereas the United States rate *rose* 6.8 percent, according to a 1992 report by The Sentencing Project, a private group promoting sentencing reform.

Many experts believe that the American system is unfair, and various groups are working to persuade the government to consider other ways of dealing with people who are accused of committing crimes. Increasingly, counties are experimenting with methods such as electronic surveillance devices to allow people to remain at home until time for their court appearance.

WAR ON DRUGS

One major factor in the staggering increase in the prison population has been the national war on drugs. Many experts believe that the program has not helped to decrease the use of drugs but only to increase the numbers in jail. Indeed, the imprisonment rate had been fairly stable throughout U.S. history until 1980. Since then, the prison and jail population has grown from 513,809 to 1,248,011 in 1991. Experts expect the growth to continue through the 1990s because of long mandatory drug sentences and cutbacks in parole. Most of the new prisoners are drug offenders. Drug arrests grew from 471,165 in 1980 to 1,089,500 in 1991.

Not only are more drug offenders going to prison, but they are receiving longer sentences. The average term served for a federal drug offense is now 60 months, versus 23 months in 1987. Some experts say that in the year 2000 one out of every 99 people in this country will live behind bars.

One of the cities with the worst prison problem is New York. In that city alone, more than 22,000 men, women, and adolescents are incarcerated. Most of them are held at Rikers Island, an institution on an island in the East River. In fact, 140,000 people go through Rikers Island each year, 80 percent because they could not raise bail of $500. The bail system is widely considered unfair. Poor people go to jail while awaiting trial, before they have been found guilty. By contrast, people who can afford to pay bail are released and allowed to be free until their case is heard in court.

Once sentenced, however, people from every income level and ethnic group are represented in the prisons.

NOT EVERYONE IN JAIL IS GUILTY

According to our laws, a person is presumed innocent until found guilty by a judge or jury. Also according to our laws, however, the police can arrest anyone who they have good reason to believe may have committed a crime. It is then up to the courts to decide whether in fact the person probably committed a crime. The *conviction* (finding of guilty) must be *beyond a reasonable doubt*. That is very important. In the United States the person accused does not have to prove innocence; rather, the district attorney (the lawyer representing the people) must prove the defendant guilty.

Shawn's father was released within a few days because a judge decided that there was not sufficient evidence to charge him with a crime.

That is not always the case. It may take much longer for people to know their chances of being released or sentenced to time in prison. The court system is very complicated. Many things have to take place before someone actually goes to court. For example, if Shawn's father had not been released at his arraignment, a court date would have been set. Very seldom is everything ready at the first court date. In such case the hearing is adjourned or postponed and a new date set. There may be many adjournments before a final court date.

This situation is difficult for the accused, because not knowing what is going to happen is harder than knowing— even when what one knows will happen is bad. Many inmates say that the time they spend in jail during court proceedings is much harder than the sentence they have had to serve, because of the uncertainty. After sentencing, at least they have a fairly good idea when they can expect to return home. In addition, their family knows what to expect and can make plans.

After an arrest, a lawyer is assigned. It can be a private lawyer if the person can afford one; otherwise, the court appoints a lawyer. The lawyer then needs time to gather information and plan a defense. Shawn's father retained a private attorney, who represented him at the arraignment. The lawyer argued that the evidence was insufficient to hold his client, and the judge agreed.

THE LAW

Criminal laws or codes define what types of conduct are criminal and establish penalties for such behavior. In the United States each state sets its own criminal laws within the guidelines laid down by the Constitution and sets penalties for violating them. About 90 percent of all criminal cases are under the jurisdiction of the lower or minor trial courts, which are generally empowered to hear misdemeanors—cases punishable by a maximum penalty of a fine or one year in jail. Major trial courts hear felony cases—more serious crimes punishable by a sentence of at least one year in prison. Federal courts hear criminal cases that involve constitutional issues such as civil rights, or offenses against federal laws such as the banking laws.

When police officers have probable cause (enough evidence) to believe that a person has violated a law, they can make an arrest. (In some jurisdictions a grand jury may be convened to decide whether there is probable cause and an arrest should be made.) Arrested persons are generally taken into police custody (in the local jail) until arraignment. At the arraignment the charges are formally filed with the court and read to the defendant (the person accused). The defendant is informed of his or her rights and assigned a lawyer if he or she does not already have one. His or her plea (guilty or not guilty) is entered. By a plea of guilty, the defendant waives the right to a trial and may be sentenced by a judge there and then. If the accused pleads not guilty, a trial date is set.

The defendant may then be released on his or her own recognizance: that is, he or she signs an agreement to appear at all court hearings. He or she may be released on posting of a money or property bond called a bail bond. Bail is forfeited if the defendant does not appear at all appointed court hearings. Defendants may pay the full amount of the bond themselves, get help from family and friends, or pay a bail-bond agent. Bail-bond agents post the full amount of the bond in exchange for a nonrefundable fee, usually 10 percent of the bond. Bail privileges may be withheld from persons accused of murder or treason. If an accused is judged to be violent, has been arrested many times, or is likely to commit new crimes if released, the judge may refuse bail or set bail so high that the accused could not afford to pay it and thus would have to stay in jail. The judge may also deny bail if the accused has an outstanding warrant for failure to appear in court for another case.

It is important to remember that people go to jail before they have been found guilty of a crime. Many things can happen after they have been arrested. They can be released because there is not sufficient evidence to hold them; they can be placed on probation; they can be fined or sentenced to community service, or they can be held in jail to await trial. Some stay in jail only a few days, others for more than a year before their case is decided.

WHAT HAPPENS IN JAIL

Once people are sent to jail, or incarcerated, they are called inmates. Jails are often large structures with many sections. Each section is called a house. Some of these houses are made up of separate cells, small rooms with bars in front of them, housing one inmate or sometimes two or three. Each cell has a sink, a toilet, and beds. Inmates are usually allowed to leave their cell and walk around other parts of the house. Often there is a dayroom, with tables, chairs, and a television set. Usually inmates are allowed to shower daily. Other houses are dormitories, large rooms with forty or fifty beds, a shower room, and a dayroom. Dormitories look somewhat like army barracks.

Inmates are watched by corrections officers, who are like police officers without guns. Their major job is to keep everyone safe. Jails are operated somewhat like the military. The staff includes officers, captains, deputy wardens, and the warden. The warden is in charge of the institution. Inmates are required to walk in straight lines through the hallways when they are going to other parts of the jail and to do as they are told in order to keep the buildings safe and orderly. Because the jails are crowded and inmates are often angry and tense, jails can be violent places and people can get hurt. Most people try to stay to themselves and do not get hurt. When someone is hurt, doctors in the jail take care of them.

Services Available

Most jails have services for inmates. They usually have a law library, where people can learn about the law and help their lawyer in their own defense. There is usually a barber shop, and a yard where they are allowed to exercise at least one hour a day. Inmates receive three meals a day, usually in a cafeteria. Each building also has a commissary, a store where inmates can purchase items such as toothpaste, cookies, and soda. The commissary holds money that inmates are sent from home or earn when they are allowed to work inside the jail. If their crime is not too serious, inmates may work cleaning the jail, in the cafeteria, in the various shops, or outside, cutting grass or doing other gardening chores.

Most large jails have a medical clinic staffed with doctors, nurses, and other professionals. Persons entering the jail are given a complete physical examination. If any illnesses are identified, the medical staff treat them. If a health problem arises with an inmate, or if someone is hurt, the medical staff responds. For this reason, many people who could not afford medical care on the outside leave jail healthier than they entered. The medical clinics often have psychiatrists and other mental health clinicians and counselors. Inmates with serious mental illness are usually quickly identified by the medical staff and sent to the mental health clinicians for treatment. In some jails, when inmates need counseling, they are assigned to a counselor whom they can see frequently. Most jails have someone on staff to whom inmates' families can talk if they are worried about their loved one. The inmate's attorney can help in finding such a person.

Visits

Inmates are entitled to have visitors, usually once or twice a week. These visits are usually held in large rooms with many other inmates and their families. Even small children may visit. Usually inmates look forward to visits and feel better after them. However, not all inmates want their family to visit them in jail. They can be embarrassed or too upset to see anyone. Some parents do not want their children to see them in jail. They may choose to talk on the phone or to write letters instead. Parents may be ready to see a child after they have had some time to adjust. Parents may worry that it is too difficult for their family to get to the jail, or that their family or children may be afraid or may have to go through too much humiliation.

Usually, all visitors are searched for any contraband, or illegal articles. No cameras, recording devices, or weapons are allowed into the jail. Each jail has its own policies; however, it is usually not permitted to give anything directly to an inmate during a visit, and there are many restrictions on what can be left for a inmate during a visit. For example, inmates are not allowed to have clothing the same color as the officers' uniforms. No drugs are allowed, including medication. Only the clinic doctor may prescribe medication for inmates. Inmates are entitled to send and receive mail. Inmates are allowed to use the telephone, usually once a day, although sometimes it is hard to get a turn. Sometimes inmates try to control the phones, and it may not be wise to fight over it.

Barbara

Barbara's sixteenth birthday party was suddenly canceled when her mother received a phone call from her father saying that he had just been arrested. He was being held at the police station for allegedly raping a neighbor's child. Barbara and her mother were both in shock.

Mrs. Baxter immediately called their lawyer, who arranged to meet her husband at the police station. The following day the lawyer called and told them that Mr. Baxter had been arraigned and that the judge had ruled there was enough evidence to keep him in custody until a trial date could be set. Apparently, the neighbor girl told her mother that Mr. Baxter had been touching her genitals. The police interviewed the girl and several people who had seen Mr. Baxter talking with the girl. They believed they had enough evidence to arrest him. Because of the serious nature of the charge, the judge was persuaded by the district attorney to set a very high bail. It was more than Barbara's family could afford. Even the 10 percent that the bail bondsman would charge was more that they could pay.

Barbara and her mother found out from the lawyer where her father was being held and planned to visit him as soon as possible. The next day he called them from the jail and told them that Tuesday was visiting day.

Barbara was relieved when she saw her father and heard from him that he was okay, although she was worried about the bruise on his face. He told her that when he first got to the jail, another inmate attacked him and took his watch, but he didn't care about the watch. In fact, he said it would be better not to have too much with him; as long as he didn't have anything too expensive, the other inmates would probably leave him alone. A corrections officer had told him that the first few days were usually the worst. Fortunately, no one in the jail knew what he had been arrested for.

Barbara went with her mother to see the lawyer the next day, and he explained that her father would probably be in jail for a while, because it would take time to prepare his case. He said there was a chance the charges would be dropped, but for now they would prepare to go to trial. Barbara and her mother could visit him once a week and talk to him on the phone every other day. For now all they could do was hope and pray that everything would be cleared up. Barbara was allowed to stay home from school for a few days, and it helped that many of her relatives visited and tried to reassure her that her father would be okay. She was sure that eventually he would be cleared.

CHAPTER ◇ 2

What Happens on the Inside?

Peter was riding a bus that would take him to the place where his father was incarcerated. This would be his first visit, and he had more questions than he dared to ask. He had seen movies about prisons but had never known anyone who was in jail. In the movies prison seemed so frightening. It was hard to believe that Dad was in such a place. Would they hurt him? Was it true that men sometimes were raped in jail, and would that happen to his father? Would he be able to ask his father any of these questions? He didn't want Dad to think he was afraid.

His mother and older sister hadn't stopped crying since his father's arrest. His mother kept wondering what they were going to do now. She worried about paying the bills, but he thought she was even more upset about being alone. She was always afraid of being alone, and the first couple of nights with his father gone were scary. Peter was worried about how he was going to take care of his mother and sister, never mind himself, but he was most worried about his father. What was going to happen to him?

PRISONS VS. JAILS

There is an important difference between prison and jail. A prison is usually where people are confined after they have been convicted of crime. A jail is a temporary holding place before trial. Most people in jail have not been convicted of a crime; they have not yet been found guilty or not guilty of anything. Because jails house large numbers of people who are there only temporarily, the community of inmates changes frequently. Some people are there for a few days and then released. Others are there for a week, a month, or several months. Also because of their temporary nature, jails often have little in the way of rehabilitative services. Prisons have schools, drug treatment programs, various trade shops, and other facilities that jails seldom have. Jails usually provide the minimum services needed to keep prisoners safe and cared for such as medical clinics, counseling, and chaplain and legal services.

The result of all this is often large buildings with many inmates, all having little to do to occupy their time. In addition, because the population changes frequently, inmates do not get to know one another or care to; why bother when they may be gone tomorrow? In general, prisoners seldom trust one another very much. In a strange way, they are more prejudiced against each other than people on the outside are against them. Perhaps they know too well what each of them is capable of—or perhaps they have been socialized to believe that they are not to be trusted. Inmates often say that each man has to watch his own back; someone is always looking to prove himself bigger or stronger than the next man. This may be a way of gaining some control over their lives, so much of which they have lost since their arrest. The other aspect of jail life that is common to almost all prisoners is fear, arising from being unable to predict or anticipate what will happen next.

Arriving in Jail

New arrivals in a jail go through a receiving room. There they strip, shower, and are searched for weapons or drugs. They are photographed, given an inmate number, and assigned to a specific house—a cell block or dormitory. The inmate number, often called a book and case number, identifies that inmate from any others who have the same last name.

When Peter first spoke to his father on the phone, his father told him his book and case number and what house he was in. Peter's father knew that it was important for his family to have this information so that they could find him in the large jail and be able to send him mail or money. When addressing mail to someone in jail, it is important to use the name under which the person was arrested, the book and case number, and the house within the jail. Sometimes, to protect their privacy, inmates do not use their real names in jail.

After processing, inmates are often taken to the medical clinic for a physical examination. Doctors take a medical history and a mental health history. They ask whether the inmates have ever been in a psychiatric hospital, have ever had emotional problems or are having problems now. They especially ask about thoughts of suicide. If the doctors are doubtful about inmates' adjusting to the jail, they refer them to other mental health professionals for counseling and protection. If the problems are serious, inmates are sent to a nearby hospital or other facility where they can get the care they need. By law, the state must care for the medical and psychiatric needs of inmates.

If family members are worried about an inmate, they may be able get the name of the doctor who is treating him or her. They can ask their lawyer for assistance or call the jail and ask to speak with the doctor or mental health person in charge.

Often the first week in jail is the hardest time. For some inmates, this is because they are deprived of the drugs they were taking or because just before their arrest they were sick and not taking very good care of themselves. Inmates who come into jail on drugs are often detoxified under medical supervision and receive medications that will help them withdraw from the drugs, just as if they had been admitted to a hospital. In some facilities, people who come in on methadone or other drugs that were prescribed by a doctor can continue those medications for as long as necessary. This is why people are examined when they first come into the jail. For many inmates, this is the first time they have received such medical attention. It may be their first chance to get the attention they need and perhaps begin to get their lives back on track. Many inmates say that in a way they are glad they were arrested, because if they hadn't been forced to stop the drugs they would soon have been dead. Some get off of drugs for the first time in their lives.

JACK'S FATHER

Jack's father, Philip Fields, had been addicted to cocaine and heroin for three years before he was arrested. His family had watched him slowly change into someone they hardly recognized. He stayed out later and later at night until he stopped coming home at all. When he was at home he slept, sometimes for days at a time. He was angered easily and began to mistrust everyone. He always acted as if someone were after him. Strange people would come to the house, and Philip would get angry whenever his son asked about them. Jack knew his father was doing drugs but dared not speak to him about it. He had prayed that something would stop his father, give him back the father he remembered, and now something had!

When Jack and his mother first visited Philip in jail, they saw a different person. His father apologized for the way things had been and promised that they would be different from now on. For the first time in three years, they were talking to the man they used to know, a man without the influence of drugs. Although they wished that there had been a better way to accomplish this, they were glad that the roller coaster of drug use had finally stopped—even if they weren't sure it was permanent.

This is often what happens when people are arrested. They are forced to stop and examine their lives, realizing that their way of life has led to only one place, jail. They regret having disappointed their families and others who love and depend on them, and they worry about their children. In addition, they can begin to think properly again when they are out from under the influence of drugs. In a strange way, Philip's arrest was a blessing both for him and his family. At least, now there was a chance for change. All crisis brings about the opportunity for change.

Problems of Jail

Even Philip Field realized this, although jail was a hard way to learn the lesson. Besides the advantages, there were many problems. Jail itself is a very difficult place to be. It is not easy for grown men or women to have every minute of their lives regulated. They are told when to wake up, when to eat meals, when to go to sleep. They are told what they can wear, when they can use the phone, what they can eat. They have to walk in lines, obey the officers, and submit to searches. Some officers abuse their authority and take advantage of prisoners; some inmates take advantage of each other. For example, an inmate who wants to exert power in the house may try to force other inmates to wash his clothes, give him their commissary items (cigarettes, candy, soda, etc.), or even have sex with him. Other inmates may have to fight him to prove that they will not be pushed around. Some inmates are able to talk their way out of conflicts or learn to act in such a way that no one approaches them.

Philip Field wanted his son to know the bad things about jail so that he would never have to find out for himself. Jack asked why his father didn't tell the officers about what went on so that these men would leave his father alone. Philip explained that it was an unspoken rule in the jail culture never to tell on another inmate. If an inmate broke this rule, the others would get him for sure. There is a strong code of secrecy in jail, and a phrase often heard is, "Snitches get stitches." In some facilities, men who "snitch" are cut on the side of the face, marking them as a snitch wherever they go in the system. Each inmate has to find his own way of defending himself within the system.

In other ways, inmates often help each other. It is not

unusual for stronger inmates to stand up for and protect those who are weaker or disabled in some way. Older men sometimes take younger inmates under their wing and teach them how to get along. Inmates who can read and write often help others by reading letters from home or writing letters for them. They sometimes give each other cigarettes or other articles, although often not without a price. For example, an inmate may give another a pack of cigarettes but expect two or three back in return. If the other inmate cannot pay up within a short time he may get hurt or have to pay in some other way. Many experienced inmates teach the younger ones not to depend on anyone else and especially not to become indebted to anyone in the jail. It is generally better to do without rather than to owe someone.

It often takes a week or longer for money sent to an inmate to get into his commissary account, which is another reason the first few weeks can be the hardest. Other articles new prisoners often need are toothpaste, shampoo, snacks, letter-writing supplies, and often clothing. Usually they have only the clothes they were arrested in and need a change of clothes while it is being washed and dried. Often inmates wash their clothes in the sink and hang it to dry in their cell.

A Jail Cell

The inmate's cell is a very small room with bars on the windows and in the door. The bars are often controlled electronically by the officers of the house, enabling them to control the movement of inmates, and also offering inmates some degree of protection from each other. However, it is not unusual for one inmate to sneak into the cell of another while the officers are not watching. Dorms sometimes offer more protection because they are open spaces and easier to monitor.

The showers are often the scene of fights, sometimes over sexual activity, sometimes because it is the only place where the officers are lax in watching.

Cells usually have a toilet, a sink, and sometimes a desk or small table for writing. The lights are controlled by the officers and turned off at a set time. Jails differ, but in many the inmates are allowed to decorate their cell or the area around their dorm bed with pictures from home, magazines, or pictures that they draw. Sometimes the pictures are pornographic, since that may be their only sexual outlet. Usually, conjugal visits (during which prisoners may visit in private with their spouse) are not allowed until inmates have been sentenced and sent to state prison. In some cases conjugal visits are never permitted; prisoners have to do the best they can to satisfy their need for intimacy with letters, telephone calls, and brief visits in a crowded room.

Danger Spots

Other dangerous places are the cafeteria, the yard, the gym, and open areas where inmates from different houses may be mixed. If two inmates have a "beef" with each other, the corrections officers often put them in separate houses. But it can be difficult to insure that they are kept apart, and fights do break out between rival inmates, or rival gangs within the jail. Jail is a microcosm of the larger society, and prejudices and other conflicts sometimes cause one group to fight another group. Hispanics may be fighting African-Americans, or either group may attack the whites. At other times all groups seem to get along without difficulty.

Sometimes fights break out between inmates and officers. Usually this is related to some prison policy that the inmates consider unfair. In other cases a small group of officers break the rules or treat inmates cruelly or unjustly. This results in fighting or, in the worst case, riots. Usually these things occur because some inmates feel powerless to change what they perceive as unfair or unjust treatment.

Corrections officers often come from the same communities as the inmates. They often have only a high school diploma, and they are sometimes required to work long hours of overtime in order to fill in for officers who are on sick leave or because of budget cuts that reduce the staff.

Under these conditions, and under the pressures, fears, and tensions in the jail, corrections officers can become irritable and angry and react in ways that are unnecessarily cruel or violent. Officers too are affected by being in the jail. Everyone inside the walls is afraid in one way or another. In addition, jails and prisons are run along military lines, and staff members are often punished or reprimanded for making a slight mistake or breaking some regulation. This makes for situations that are difficult for officers and inmates alike.

More of Jack's Questions

As Jack heard all this, he had even more questions. Why do the jails have to be such terrible places? He spoke to his Uncle Bob about it. Jack's uncle, his father's brother, was someone with whom he felt comfortable asking questions that he would not ask any other adult. Ever since Jack was born, Uncle Bob had been very close to him, sometimes almost closer than his own father. He had never been in jail, and he was angry with his brother for continuing to do drugs and for getting arrested.

Uncle Bob told Jack that jails were not meant to be country clubs. They were places to keep society safe from men like his brother. "If he couldn't do the time, he shouldn't have done the crime."

This, of course, did not make Jack feel any better. He did not like thinking of his father as someone who had to be behind bars for other people to be safe. Jack did not feel unsafe around his father most of the time.

Some of what Uncle Bob said was true. What he failed to mention, however, were some factors that help to explain why we have so many jails and why jails are the way they are. Bob did not mention that when Philip first lost his job he tried for six months to find work in construction, but there were no jobs. People were short of money and afraid of losing their job, so they were not buying houses. Jack's father tried to keep up his spirits; however, as the weeks and months passed it became harder and harder to feel good about himself or to find things to do to occupy his time. He felt ashamed that he could not buy things for his family.

As his depression became harder to cope with, Jack's father began hanging out on the street and then tried using cocaine. The cocaine helped him forget his problems. After a while, he began using heroin and then crack. Soon he was out of control and needed money to support his drug habit. He had begun his journey to jail.

Some people like Uncle Bob would argue that many people are out of work and not all of them end up in jail, that Philip could have prevented it if he were a different sort of person. Jack could also speak with others who would see it differently. They would say that in a society that offered solutions for people with problems, Jack's father would have had a better chance of getting help and might not have resorted to drugs to cope with his situation.

Whatever the case, the truth is that everyone is different and finds different ways of coping with their difficulties depending on the resources available to them, what they have learned, or what they are used to in their personal lives. No matter what the reasons were for Philip Field's dilemma, another truth is that he now has another opportunity. He must survive the experience of being locked up and all that goes on in jail. But he has an opportunity to reexamine his life, and he has options open to him to get help in the jail or prepare for getting help when he is released. The immediate question for Jack's father and his family at present is what will happen to his court case. Will he be released, put on probation, or sentenced to time in prison.

CHAPTER ◇ 3

Visiting

Every jail is different, but most have several things in common. The jail may be in an out-of-the-way place. Visiting days are limited, and many regulations govern visiting procedures. Items called contraband may not be taken into the jail. Other items such as food and cigarettes are allowed, but they have to be purchased by the inmate at the commissary, and may not be brought to inmates by visitors. Other items such as clothing, pictures, and personal items can be brought during a visit, but they must be turned over to the officers to be searched and x-rayed before being given to the inmate. Money has to be put into the inmate's commissary account, which he can draw on like a bank account.

Because of security concerns, visitors are often searched before they can enter the visiting room. Jails have varying lists of contraband, but certain things are forbidden everywhere. Some things are obvious, such as weapons and drugs; others are not so obvious, such as cameras, tape recorders, or chewing gum. Contraband found during a visit is confiscated. If it is illegal, such as drugs, the visitors risk arrest themselves. Corrections officers are authorized to make arrests, although it is not their major function. Corrections officers carry guns, but not in jails.

Cameras and tape recorders are prohibited to protect the privacy of prisoners and sometimes the officers. In addition, pictures can be used to plan escapes. Chewing gum can be used to make locks inoperable.

Often there are restrictions on the color of clothing that can be given to inmates. They are not allowed to wear clothing that could be mistaken for the officers' uniforms. For example, blue shirts and pants may not be worn where the officers' uniforms are blue. Often jail captains wear white shirts (they are often called "white shirts"), so white shirts are not allowed. Since jail prisoners are awaiting trial and have not been convicted of a crime, they have more rights than convicted prisoners, who usually wear uniforms.

It should be kept in mind when taking clothes to someone in jail that inmates can get into trouble having expensive articles that other inmates may want. Inmates who flaunt jewelry or high-style sneakers are often considered the toughest because they were able to keep these things. At times conditions in jail can get so bad that even the gold in a inmate's teeth may be taken. They often cannot wear any of their own belongings. Instead they wear only the jail uniform. For these reasons, when people are arrested wearing jewelry or expensive clothing, they are often encouraged to turn over their property for safekeeping until they are released or transferred to other facilities.

The Visiting Room

Visits are usually held in large rooms with many families visiting at the same time. In some jails they are held in booths with a plexiglass glass window between the visitor and the inmate and an intercom (usually looking like a phone) by which the two people can communicate. Booths may be used for inmates who have broken visiting rules, or who have a contagious disease.

Visitors may not be allowed to have any physical contact with inmates for many reasons. For one thing, they could pass along drugs or other contraband. For example, an inmate may talk a visitor into bringing drugs in a plastic bag and passing it along through a kiss. They may want visitors to bring drugs for other reasons than their own use. They may be being pressured by other inmates to get drugs as payment for protection or other favors, or to avoid being hurt. Whatever the reason, it is never a good idea for family members to comply with these requests, as they too may be arrested or may not be allowed to visit again.

Visiting is also difficult for many emotional reasons. It is upsetting to see your parent in jail. It is painful to have such a limited time to talk and then have to leave the person in jail. Sometimes the visit can produce a lot of crying or other strong emotions. When possible, however, it is best to express your feelings rather than keeping them inside. Although emotions can be very frightening, they never kill. It is better to face your feelings and express them than to run from them or try to deny them. Often it can be an emotional relief to see that your parent or loved one is holding up well.

In general, visiting is safe. Everything in the jail is monitored and regimented, and officers are always present. In addition, inmates look forward to visits, so they are careful not to break any rules that would end the visit.

Like anything else involving human beings, however, nothing is certain, and occasionally fighting or other disturbances break out. It could be caused by an inmate's

VISITING ◇ 27

looking at or flirting with another inmate's visitor. It can be the result of frustration between inmates and their visitors, or problems between inmates and officers or visitors and officers. Inmates sometimes hear news from visitors that they do not want to hear and that upsets them. It is painful for parents to have lost control of their family, and sometimes the person in jail overreacts to make up for feeling out of control. Loss of control, both of oneself and of others, is perhaps the hardest thing for inmates and prisoners to accept when they are behind bars and every aspect of their lives is controlled by others. As a result, they may try to run the lives of their family, leading to arguments and hurt feelings.

Other inmates have an opposite reaction. They don't want their family to suffer, to have to keep visiting or put their lives on hold while they wait for the inmate to get out of jail. So they tell loved ones to forget about them, or not to visit anymore. Sometimes this mood passes and they change their mind, but other times this is the way they choose it to be. For some inmates, it is too much to worry about their families and loved ones and at the same time worry about themselves, their safety, and their court case. Other inmates may simply be too depressed or too anxious to concentrate on anything or anyone.

During a visit you might become worried about your parent's state of mind. For example, your father might talk about suicide or seem more upset than you expected. If so, talk to someone in charge and ask for help. Jails have doctors, counselors, or concerned officers to whom you can talk by phone after a visit. They will make sure that someone checks up on your parent.

The security procedures involved in a visit may be difficult in themselves. For example, inmates are often stripped and searched before and after every visit. They may be required to wear plain overalls to prevent them from hiding any contraband they might have received. If a visitor or an inmate breaks any of the rules, the visit will be ended. In addition, the inmate may be punished by being put in solitary confinement and being denied privileges.

TO VISIT OR NOT TO VISIT

Yolanda

Not everybody is ready to visit a parent or loved one in jail. Yolanda is seventeen, and her father had been incarcerated several times in her life. She was used to the routine of visiting, and the difficulties discussed above were not what bothered her. Yolanda's problem was deciding whether or not she wanted to visit her father this time around.

She had lived most of her life without much of a relationship with her father. He had been in prison several times, the first time for two years, then seven years. He had never been at home for more than six months at a time. Even when he was home, she didn't see him much. He was always fighting with her mother. After his release from prison the last time, everything was supposed to get better, but instead it got worse. Her mother was more upset than when he was in prison, and Yolanda often saw her crying because she didn't know where he was at night or when he would be home. Yolanda couldn't imagine why her mother put up with it. She resented her father's behavior when her mother had waited so faithfully for him to get out of prison.

Yolanda hadn't always felt this way. The other times her

father had been in prison, she used to visit him occasionally, and she often wrote him letters, most of which he answered. She had a romantic image of him and what it would to be like when he finally came home. She heard so many stories from her mother about how much he loved her and what a wonderful man he was and how everything was going to be better this time when he came home.

Her father wrote her about how sorry he was that he couldn't be there to watch her grow up. He said he was going to make up for lost time when he got home. He always asked her to take good care of her mother, and he seemed so concerned about what they were going through. She couldn't help wondering why he didn't take better care of them when he was free. She felt deceived and foolish for believing his lies.

Now he was in jail again and asking to see her. What was it with him? He seemed nicer when he was in jail then when he was home. She was angry, and she was also sad. Her mother kept telling her not to think bad things about her father, and that she had to go see him because he was asking for her. How could she help what she was thinking or feeling? All those years of looking forward to things being better when he got home, and it was just one big disappointment. What was she supposed to think now? She couldn't bear the thought of starting the old visiting routine all over again.

THE POWER OF FANTASY

One thing that can happen when a parent is absent is that a gap is created, a sense of something being missing. Often, when we want something badly, we fill that gap with what we wish for, what we make up, or—another way of saying it—with our fantasies. We create a fantasy parent in our imagination to take the place of the absent parent. One nice thing about fantasies is that they become whatever we want or need them to be. What may not be so great is that when we lose touch with the fact that this is only a fantasy, we begin to live that fantasy. The real parent who returns home will not be the fantasy parent. He or she will be himself. What Yolanda, her father, and her mother were dealing with was the power of these fantasies.

Yolanda wanted more than anything to believe that her father would really take care of them when he returned home and would be there for both her and her mother. She looked forward to seeing her mother happy again and having her parents together for the first time in many years. Yolanda's mother shared these fantasies, and so they became very easy to believe.

Yolanda's father also wanted to believe that he had changed, that this time when he got home he would do things differently. All this despite the fact that in all his life the only way he knew of getting what he wanted was to take it. He didn't have much education, and he had never learned a money-making trade. In prison he didn't participate in any of the programs that might have prepared him to earn a living. Yet, like every father, he needed to feel like a man able to provide for his family. He wanted things to be different, but he hadn't done anything to make them be different.

The sad reality was that prison was where he knew best how to get along—it was where he had spent most of his adult life. It was the outside world that he had no idea how to negotiate. All the wishing in the world was not going to change the reality that his actions kept landing him back in the same place.

Yolanda was angry because she had believed her father

when he said that he was going to be home with them. This time would be different. This time she would have a harder time believing in her fantasy father. This time if she visited her father, she would be visiting the man she knew him to be. Her big question was whether she wanted to visit this man; was she prepared to face him? Her mother said, "He is your father, and no matter what he does you should want to see him." But Yolanda didn't feel that way. She wasn't sure she wanted anything to do with him.

YOU ARE ENTITLED TO YOUR FEELINGS

What Yolanda must understand is that her feelings are her own and she is entitled to them. It is perfectly understandable that she might be too disappointed in her father to want to see him at all. Or she may need more time before she is prepared to visit him. Her feelings may change over time, or they may not. Whatever they are at any given time, she can only feel what she feels. What one does can be right or wrong, but what one thinks or feels can only be what it is. When a parent goes to jail it affects everyone differently. It can be especially difficult for children, because they may feel a sense of guilt. It may seem like their fault because they feel as if they are being punished. In some sense, the whole family has been sentenced to something that will change their lives.

Yolanda's father probably didn't intend to hurt her or his wife, but he often did things without thinking of the consequences. Nevertheless, whether he intended to hurt others or not, the fact was that he did. And when someone is hurt, it is normal to feel angry or sad.

Not thinking about consequences is what prevented Yolanda's father from learning from his experiences.

Yolanda knew well what the consequences were: She also had to live with them. In fact, the consequences were what she lived with most. She was not with her father when he committed the crimes that landed him in prison. She could not know his thoughts before he did something that got him arrested, nor could she be aware of his life experiences that may have contributed to his choices. What she lived with were the consequences of his behavior. She lived with her mother's tears, her lack of a father to rely on, the family's lack of resources as they lost their breadwinner. Yolanda suffered all this and also the embarrassment of having a father in jail, the teasing of her peers, and the loss of self-esteem.

You can see why Yolanda felt hurt and angry that her father was in jail again. In fact, if she did not feel angry or disappointed, it might be worse for her. It might mean that she was not aware of her feelings, and that would be more confusing for her. As long as she was aware of what she was feeling, there was a chance she could talk to someone about it. Often only by talking about troubles can they be made better.

WHEN YOUR FATHER REFUSES A VISIT

Peter was twelve when his father was arrested for possession of stolen property. Although Steven Hunt never talked about what he was doing, Peter knew that his father was involved in something illegal. It was an unspoken rule at home: Peter never asked what his father was doing and Hunt never spoke about it. In every other way, he and his father were close. They did a lot of things together, and Peter knew that his father loved him very much.

Peter also knew that his father was always worried

about finances. There never was enough money at home, and his father worked very hard at odd jobs: fixing things for people, painting houses, buying broken electronic devices, fixing them, and selling them to friends and neighbors. It seemed that his father never rested. Peter often heard him talking on the phone about money, and he knew that his father was constantly worried about paying the rent and having enough money for food.

One day Steven met some men and brought them to the house. Peter had a bad feeling about these men, probably because his father always seemed worried when they came over. It turned out that these men were committing robberies and were paying Steven to hide the stolen property and to sell it for them. One day the police turned up at the house and Steven was arrested and taken away in handcuffs. His sister, Aunt Betty, came to live in the house and take care of Peter.

Peter asked Aunt Betty if they could visit his father. Peter wanted to be sure he was all right and to talk to him. Aunt Betty said she would see, but after she received a phone call from Steven she said that his father wasn't ready to see anyone. Peter's father was ashamed to face his son or anyone in the family. He was embarrassed and did not want anyone, especially Peter, to see him in jail. Steven didn't know what to say to his son. He needed time to think. How could he explain what had happened? How could he admit that he had broken the law when he was always telling his son to follow the rules?

One of the reasons Steven had never spoken about what was he was doing was that he didn't want his son to know. He was afraid that Peter would think less of him, or conclude that it was okay to do something illegal. Yet at the same time, Steven felt trapped. He knew no other way of getting the money he needed to take care of Peter: school expenses, doctor and dentist bills, clothing, food, rent, activities that had to be paid for. Steven couldn't bear to tell Peter that they couldn't afford a movie or the latest in sneakers. So he agreed to a deal that he knew was wrong because he felt he needed the money. Some people get caught up in mistakes because they cannot see alternatives, and then they have to pay the consequences.

Peter was lucky. Aunt Betty was kind and understanding, and she spent a lot of time talking to him about his father. She was not afraid to answer all his questions. She explained to Peter that Steven refused to let Peter visit not because he didn't love Peter or want to see him, but because he wasn't ready to face him. Being arrested for the first time is a very traumatic event. Arrest is a crisis, and it may take people a long time to find a way of coping with that crisis, of working through the many feelings aroused by being arrested, such as confusion and fear. Often they are most embarrassed with the people that they care about the most, those that they fear they have disappointed the most. Parents especially know that they have let down their child who may always have seen them as perfect, and it may take them time to prepare what they will say and how they will explain things.

Aunt Betty suggested that Peter write his father a letter and tell him everything he was feeling. She warned him that his father might not feel able to answer right away but said she was sure he would appreciate the letter anyway. More important, it would be helpful for Peter to express his thoughts and feelings toward his father.

Peter took his aunt's advice and sat down to write to his father. He wrote that he missed him and was worried about him and that he hoped to be able to visit him, although he understood that he might not be able to do

VISITING ◇ 35

that soon. He said that he was doing fine, that Aunt Betty was taking good care of him, and that his father need not worry about him. He wrote that he hoped his father would be safe and that he missed him. He asked what was going to happen next. Would his father be going to court, and could he, Peter, be there to see for himself what might happen? He ended saying that Aunt Betty thought his father might be too embarrassed to see him. He begged his father not to be ashamed, saying that he wasn't, that he still loved him no matter what, and that he only wanted to see him.

Peter felt better after writing the letter. He hoped that his father would answer, but even if he didn't answer Peter was still glad he had said what he did.

Aunt Betty got all the information necessary to make sure the letter would reach Philip as soon as possible. She called the Legal Aid attorney assigned to the case, and the attorney gave her Philip's book and case number, the address of the jail, and his father's house in the jail. He also verified that Philip had used his right name when he was arrested so that there would be no confusion there.

Aunt Betty and Peter addressed the envelope together, and Peter mailed it. Aunt Betty said that Peter was doing the best thing for both himself and his father. She told him she was sorry he had to go through this but that it was important to keep talking about it and expressing his feelings as he had in the letter. Aunt Betty realized that when bad things happen to you, they can become even worse if you keep your thoughts and feelings to yourself. Sometimes having even one person to share things with can be very important. It wasn't easy for Peter to write that letter. In general, it is not easy for Peter to talk about things that worry him or make him feel bad. But with

Aunt Betty's encouragement and support he was able to do a very good thing for himself.

FACTS ABOUT VISITING

Jails and prisons are difficult places for everyone—the inmates, the officers, and visitors. Everyone is under pressure, people are often frightened, and all this makes people act in ways that they wouldn't normally. One thing all jails have in common is a focus on security. Most of the rules are for the purpose of insuring security. In jail security has two meanings: keeping everyone as safe as possible, and preventing prisoners from escaping. Rules are designed to keep inmates safe from each other, keep officers safe from inmates and at times inmates safe from officers, and keep visitors and other civilians who work in the jail safe from inmates.

As a rule visiting is fairly safe, partly because of the regimentation and the many rules. Usually both inmates and visitors are looking forward to the occasion, and everyone is on their best behavior. On occasion, however, problems occur. Inmates can get angry for one reason or another. They can get angry at the officers, at their visitors, and often with themselves. They may believe an officer has acted too harshly or has been insensitive to the feelings of the inmate or the visitor. They may hear things from their visitor that they would rather not hear. They may believe that another inmate is flirting with their visitor.

Whatever the case, when trouble breaks out during a visit, all visits may be terminated. In general, it is wise to follow directions without question and as promptly as possible. Problems can escalate rapidly in a jail. Officers

VISITING

may need to act quickly to bring about order, and they rarely have patience for explanations.

Visitors to a jail are asked for identification. Often this means identification with a picture attached, such as a driver's license or a passport. You can save a lot of time and nuisance by finding out the visiting rules in advance. Many visitors have spent time and money to get to the jail or prison, waited on long lines, and put up with crowds, only to find that they did not have the proper identification or had come on a day when their family member was not allowed visitors. It is always a good idea to ask a lot of questions before you visit for the first time, so that you will know what to expect and avoid as many problems as possible.

CHAPTER ◇ 4

Women Go to Jail Too

Male and female inmates face many of the same "pains of imprisonment." According to criminologist Gresham Sykes, these are first the deprivation of liberty and the loneliness and boredom of imprisonment. Second, prisoners are deprived of all goods and services from the outside world. Stripped of possessions, they often equate their material losses with personal inadequacy. The third deprivation, for the majority, is the absence of heterosexual relationships. Fourth, prisoners are subjected to a vast body of institutional regulations designed to control every aspect of their lives.

Men and women are different inside and outside of jail. Our culture encourages different things in men than in women. Wherever people live, they develop a culture, a way of being with other people. Prison is no exception. Even behind bars, cultures develop, and they are different for men than for women. Male and female prison cultures are largely influenced by role behaviors learned outside of prison. In general, women are more family-oriented, more dependent on others for relationships that make them feel safe. Although in jail they are not actually with their families, they appear to create pseudofamilies, relationships that are similar to families (although people outside of jail would hardly think of them that way). Through these pseudofamilies they try to duplicate the relationships that they miss. For example, they may call each other by familiar terms such as mother, sister, or even husband or girlfriend. This helps them to feel safe and connected to others. It satisfies needs for companionship, friendship, and love.

Sometimes this also includes homosexual relationships, but not always. When men or women have sexual relationships in jail, it is often out of need, not out of preference. After their release they return to their usual heterosexual behavior.

Members of a prison "family" are often protective of each other and look after each other the way families do on the outside. A strong woman may become the mother or the husband, so to say, of other girls and protect them the way she would her husband or children. The practice helps women survive their time in jail with less isolation. Sometimes families fight other families. Often they establish a type of stable community that protects against fighting, violence, or even rape. As a result, it is less likely for women to be raped in jail than for men.

Women are held in smaller prisons with fewer programs and recreational opportunities. The programs that are offered reflect stereotyped female roles, with emphasis on housekeeping, sewing, clerical, and typing skills. Female prison populations are growing at a faster rate than are male populations, however: 12.5 percent versus 7.1 percent in 1988. For that reason, even programs that were once available to women inmates are becoming more difficult to enter. Living conditions for women prisoners—both in women's prisons and in the women's wings of men's prisons—have grown even more onerous than conditions for men. A recent development, the co-correctional prison, permits a certain level of male-female mixing and offers improved program opportunities for women.

Overall, women enter prison with more serious health problems than men, or they may be pregnant. Mothers may have the burden of worry about the care of their children while they are in prison.

WHY WOMEN ARE IN JAIL

The public is not generally aware of women in prison. Most people think in stereotypes, generalizations that are usually not true. Somehow when a woman goes to jail it seems different because we are more used to men being arrested and imprisoned. Men tend to commit more violent and sensational crimes and so are more often in the newspapers and on TV. Most prison movies are about men.

Yet a growing proportion of women are ending up in jail, especially with the war on drugs and as the problems of poverty in our society deepen.

As a result, since there is less knowledge about women in jail, they are more subject to stereotypes. And as usual generalizations about women who get arrested are often incorrect and may be very hurtful to both the women and their families. Some people believe that women have to do something really bad, much worse than men, to be put to jail. That is not true. The truth is that most of the women in jail are there on drug-related charges. Drug sale and use are a serious problem for our society among both men and women. Since the government has chosen to deal with it by incarcerating those involved with drugs, the past twenty years have seen a huge increase in the number of men and women in prison.

As a result, more children than ever are growing up with a mother in jail.

WHEN YOUR MOTHER IS IN JAIL

Having your mother go to jail is probably one of the most difficult things that you will ever have to deal with. Your mother brings you into this world. She is the first person you love and the person who takes care of you.

Because of the special nature of this first relationship, your unconscious mind remembers being held and fed as an infant, and sometimes you feel safe with your mother or when you think of your mother because of that early experience.

What we feel, however, is not always the way things are. For example, it can feel good to sleep late in the morning, even through it would be better to get up and get to school on time. It may feel frightening to be in a dark room even though there is really nothing in the room to be afraid of. In the same way, even though we might actually be safe living with a relative or even in a foster home, it might not "feel" as safe as being with our mother. In fact, we may be *safer* with another family, even though we do not feel that way.

Take, for example, a mother who has a serious drug-abuse problem. She might fall asleep smoking and burn the house down. She might be so high that she forgets to feed you, or doesn't come home at night and leaves you alone. Yet you might "feel" safer with her simply because she is your mother than with a relative who does not have drug problems and who can actually take better care of you.

Mother Bonding

Nevertheless, no matter what the reality, you love your mother, and it feels awful when you are separated from her. You may be afraid of what will happen to you next, or what might happen to your mother. You probably miss her and want to talk to her. You may wish you could hug her and tell her that you love her.

You may be angry at her for doing something that got her arrested. You may be embarrassed and feel as if something is wrong with you because of what your mother did. Perhaps you are keeping it a secret from your friends and teachers. Maybe you are making up stories to explain where your mother is. You might even say she has died. Some children even wish that their mother *had* died, rather than gotten arrested and put in jail or prison.

It is important to remember that you are experiencing a crisis in your life. When something very upsetting happens, people don't always know what to do, or they may find themselves doing things that they wouldn't ordinarily do. You may be so upset that your usual ways of coping with difficulties don't work. You may be so frightened, so confused, or so nervous that you say the first thing that comes into your mind, or do the easiest thing to avoid the situation until you feel stronger or can better understand what has happened. You must remember that you are only human. You need to be kind and patient with yourself. Sometimes the hardest thing of all is to be good to ourselves.

Need for Support

You need a lot of support right now. You need people who will listen to you and try to understand what you are going through. Right now no one should try to tell you what you are supposed to be feeling or that anything you *are* feeling is wrong. You cannot control your feelings or thoughts, and you need to be allowed to feel your own feelings. There may be nothing that anyone could say to make you feel better at the moment. Often just listening and trying to understand is the most that anyone can do. Just that in itself can help sometimes. It hurts to feel completely alone. No one may be able to understand exactly what you are going through, but the more you can explain it to someone, the less you will feel that you are carrying the burden alone.

Perhaps you have a favorite relative or a neighbor or a teacher whom you have felt close to in the past. These are the people you should seek out and talk to. It might also be that you need to talk with a professional helper, a social worker or therapist who has experience with children in your situation. The people around you may not realize how hard this is for you. Sometimes the best thing for you to do is take the initiative, tell someone in your life that you want to see a counselor.

Asking for Help

Be prepared for the fact that adults do not always hear what you say the first time. You may need to ask many times. Some adults are afraid of counseling or don't realize that it can help. They feel that they have handled their own problems all their lives and that is how everyone should do it. They may not realize that everyone is different and needs different things. Or they may be mistaken. They may think that they are handling their own problems when they are not. They may be making the same mistakes over and over again and never learn any better.

If you keep on asking or ask other adults, perhaps someone will listen and will help you get assistance from a professional therapist. Sometimes adults forget what it is like to be a child. They forget how scary things can be. They even forget how to talk with children. If you can't get anyone in your family to listen, try a teacher or the principal. Often the best way to begin is simply to say, "I need help; can I talk to you?" If you are worried about too many people knowing what has happened, you can always ask a counselor or teacher to keep what you say confidential. That means that they promise not to tell anyone what you talk about unless they have your permission to do so.

Susan

One day Susan was called into the principal's office. She was frightened and couldn't imagine what she had done wrong. When she went into the office, a strange lady and a police officer were there. The principal said the lady was a social worker and they wanted to talk to her. Susan had heard about social workers, and she didn't like them. Her friends talked about social workers who took kids away from their families. She felt like crying, but she couldn't let anyone see that she was afraid, so she began to act tough and didn't say anything. Then came the bad news: Her mother had been arrested for selling drugs, and Susan would have to go with the social worker until they could find a place for her to live.

Her worst fear had come true. She had known her mother was taking drugs, and she worried that something might happen to her. Now it had. Susan wanted to cry, but she held the tears back. At first she refused to go with the social worker. She said she was fourteen and could take care of herself. The principal and the social worker told her that it was against the law for children under eighteen to be without parental guidance.

Susan didn't feel the need for any guidance. She was the one who took care of her mother. She did most of the shopping and the cooking. She took care of herself at home, decided when to go to bed, how to dress, what to eat. Plenty of times she was alone all night and sometimes for two days at a time. What was the big deal? She didn't understand.

Susan was a "parentified child," one who assumes the parenting role and takes care of her mother instead of her mother's taking care of her. Parentified children often grow up too fast. They feel that they don't need anyone, that they can take care of themselves. In fact, they often feel special in being responsible for their parents.

Deep down, however, Susan knew that she was frightened and very upset. Although she felt grown-up, she really was still a child. All children need someone that they can go to, that they can depend on to tell them what to do, explain things they may not understand, cook and care for them so that they can concentrate on what is important at fourteen. Susan was missing out on a major part of life. Her energy should have been directed toward school, learning, friends, and playing. It had been a long time since she had been able to focus on those things. Now she was going to live with adults who would try to enable her to do so.

Although in some ways that might have been better for

Susan, it didn't feel that way to her at the time. What was she going to do? Most important, when would she see her mother, and when would they get back together?

But things did not turn out as badly as Susan had expected. The social worker, Ms. Beard, investigated and found out that Susan's grandmother would be glad to take care of her. The grandmother lived in the next town, but Susan had not seen her since Susan's mother began taking drugs. Susan remembered her from a long time ago, but she didn't remember how nice her grandmother was.

A New Home

When she got to her grandmother's house, she found a bedroom all prepared for her and a meal waiting. A real meal—spaghetti and meat balls, bread, and salad. Susan hadn't sat down to a real meal for some time, and she had never had a room all to herself. Her grandmother greeted her with a big hug and cried a little when she said how happy she was to see her. It felt kind of nice to be with her grandmother. Her arms were so strong, and for a moment Susan felt safe. Her grandmother even smelled nice. Susan had never known someone could smell so nice. After dinner there was ice cream and they watched TV.

Susan felt guilty being so contented with her grandmother. She thought she wasn't supposed to be happy about anything with her mother in jail. She felt that if she got to love her grandmother or, even worse, liked living there, she would be betraying her mother. After all, no matter what her mother had done she was still her mother. And she always used to tell Susan that no one would ever love her the way she did. Her mother always said it was just the two of them; no one else could ever understand each other the way they did. What would happen if her mother found out that she actually liked being with her grandmother?

Ms. Beard visited a few day later and asked how things were going. Susan said everything was fine and asked when she would be able to see her mother. The social worker said soon but asked again if everything was okay. She could tell that something was bothering Susan. When Susan refused to say anything, Ms. Beard said, "You know, Susan, some children in your situation feel guilty about liking where they are. They think they will disappoint their mother if they feel good about how someone is taking care of them." Susan just listened.

Ms. Beard explained that Susan's mother had many problems. In some ways, she needed to be taken care of herself, so she couldn't really take care of Susan at this time. She asked if Susan had any younger friends or cousins. Susan said she had a friend named Cheryl, who was only ten. Cheryl lived at home with both her parents. When Susan was younger, Cheryl's mother used to babysit for her.

Ms. Beard asked Susan to imagine what it might be like if Cheryl's parents were arrested. Would she want Cheryl to be alone? If Cheryl enjoyed being taken care of by her grandmother, do you think that would make Cheryl bad? Susan answered, "Of course not." She wouldn't want Cheryl to be all alone.

Sometimes it is easier to understand what other children need or might feel under certain circumstances than to admit the same things about ourselves. Susan could understand that there would be nothing wrong with Cheryl's living with her grandmother; after all, it wouldn't have been her fault if her parents were gone. "The same is true of you," Ms. Beard told Susan. "It isn't your fault that your mother was arrested. You can't be expected to act as a parent for your mother. Adults are supposed to know how to take care of themselves, but children are not. It's only natural to feel good if someone is taking care of you." Susan was half convinced.

The social worker asked Susan to imagine one more story. "Suppose you had a pet, say a puppy about eight months old, and you had to go away for a year. Wouldn't you want someone nice to take care of the puppy? And wouldn't you want your puppy to be as happy as it could while you were gone?" When Susan nodded, Ms. Beard asked softly, "Don't you think you are at least as important as a puppy, or your friend Cheryl?"

Susan began to feel a little better. As time went on, she lived with her grandmother and saw Ms. Beard about twice a month. Eventually she got to visit her mother.

With the help of her grandmother and her social worker, Susan eventually learned not to feel guilty about what happened to her mother. She even learned not to feel guilty about enjoying living with her grandmother. It was always hard to think about her mother in jail, and not to be with her when she wanted to be, but Susan learned that it was okay to feel bad about that. Susan needed to do the best she could with her own life.

One good thing did come out of Susan's mother's prison term. Like many crises, it became an opportunity for change. First, she got off drugs. When she began to think more clearly, she talked with the counselors and started attending Narcotics Anonymous meetings in the prison. She has been off drugs for over a year now, and she hopes to be free in about four years.

Susan and her mother have been talking a lot about their feelings for each other. Susan feels hopeful that when her mother returns home, they will have a better relationship. She still feels depressed sometimes, and it is still difficult when people ask where her mother is, but Susan is learning to deal with that. She has learned to be selective about her friends. Real friends understand and are supportive of Susan. Those who don't understand, she doesn't talk to about this. She has learned to decide whom to tell, and whom not to tell.

CHAPTER ◇ 5

What Will Happen in Court

Ali was very excited that his father was finally going to court today. His father had been in jail for a month since his arrest for gun possession. When Ali had visited yesterday, his father told him about the court date and that the judge might release him right away. Ali, his mother, his sisters, and his grandmother all went to the courthouse. They looked at the court calendar posted on the wall and found his father's name and the section of the courthouse he would be in. They asked a court clerk where that was, and they sat patiently in the courtroom waiting for his father to appear.

The hours passed, and many cases were called. Late in the day, Ali's father finally appeared. Two minutes later he was on his way back to jail. Ali and his family were shocked. They didn't understand what had happened.

What happened to Ali happens to many families when they do not know what to expect. His father's attorney was not ready to proceed with the case and therefore

WHAT WILL HAPPEN IN COURT?

asked for an adjournment. The hearing was rescheduled for the next month. Before a case is settled, there may be many adjournments. It can take months, sometimes more than a year, before a case is finally decided. The defendant's lawyer needs time to meet and discuss the matter with the client and then prepare the case. At the same time the prosecutor—the district attorney or assistant district attorney—also needs time to prepare. He or she needs to talk with witnesses, prepare legal arguments, and file many types of papers.

PLEA BARGAINING

Often, the prosecutor and the defense attorney (the defendant's lawyer) may need to talk. If the defendant pleads guilty, they need time to prepare a "plea," which is an agreement on how long a sentence will be asked. For example, the defense attorney might tell Ali's father that he doesn't think he can win the case and that the district attorney has offered to ask the judge for five to ten years for a plea of guilty. In that case there will be no trial. Instead, the parties go before the judge and propose the deal. If the judge agrees, Ali's father will be sentenced to a minimum of five years and a maximum of ten years. Ali's father can be released after about five years if he doesn't get into any trouble in prison and if the Parole Board believe that he is ready to leave prison. Sometimes the sentence includes "time served"; if the person has already been in jail six months and the sentence is one and a half to three years, he or she could get out in six to eight months. Also, time in jail often counts more than normal time.

If the defendant decides to go to trial, it can take much longer. Preparation can take months, and the trial itself can take several weeks. In the meantime, the family may have to go back and forth to court many times, never knowing which time something important will happen.

LEGAL INSANITY

In addition to waiting for probation and parole reports, many other things can cause a case to be adjourned. One delay arises if the judge or one of the lawyers thinks that the defendant has serious psychological or emotional problems. The judge may believe that the defendant is not "competent to participate in his own defense" or is legally insane.

Not being competent to participate in the defense means that the accused cannot understand how courts operate. For example, he or she may not understand the role of the judge, the prosecutor, or the defense attorney. He may not understand that the defense attorney is there to help him and that he should cooperate in order to protect his rights.

If someone in the court believes that this might be the case, the defendant is examined by a court-appointed psychiatrist. This is usually called an Article 730 exam. If the person fails the 730 exam, which means he has been found incompetent to stand trial, he is sent to a forensic psychiatric hospital to be treated. When his condition is improved and he can understand enough to cooperate with the defense, he then must stand trial.

If the defendant is found legally insane, it means that at the time of the crime he or she was too ill mentally to know that it was wrong. In such a case the person is committed to a state forensic facility until the doctors find he is no longer sick and can be returned to the community. A person found legally insane is not held responsible for the crime but is too dangerous to be out in the community. The law allows him or her to be committed indefinitely for psychiatric treatment until doctors are reasonably sure that he or she has been cured.

Sometimes people are really sick, and these procedures are necessary to protect both the defendant and everyone else. Sometimes people pretend to be sick to avoid having to go to jail. Psychiatric evaluations can take a long time, because the doctors have to be sure whether the person is really sick or pretending.

APPEALS

You should realize that the legal system, like any system run by human beings, can be flawed. The people in the system can make mistakes. Decisions are always the opinions of the people in charge. That means that sometimes innocent people are convicted of crimes and can be sentenced and serve time in jail for things they did not do. Likewise, people who are guilty can be acquitted.

For this reason, the legal system allows for appeals. A defendant who is found guilty has the right to appeal the case to a higher court. The judges on that court read the transcript of the case (a written record of everything that was said in the courtroom) and decide whether or not all the defendant's rights were protected and the trial was properly conducted. In effect, they decide whether the judge made any mistakes while hearing the case.

The judge is responsible for making sure that everything that happens in the course of a trial is legal and everyone's rights have been protected. Sometimes judges make mistakes. It sometimes happens that after someone has been found guilty and has served a number of years in prison, the case goes to appeal. The higher court finds that the person's rights were not protected and orders a new trial. At the new trial, the defendant may be found not guilty and be released.

What all of this means is that you and your parent should not give up hope if your parent is sentenced to prison. There are still other legal recourses. Your parent might win on appeal, or the sentence could be reduced and your parent be freed earlier than expected. However, the appeal process takes a long time, often many years, and everyone needs to be very patient while waiting for the result.

COURT CAN BE A BATTLE

The Prosecution

If your parent decides to plead not guilty, the case then goes to trial. If you are going to attend the trial, you need to be aware that it can be a very painful process. There are two sides to every trial. It is the job of the prosecution to prove that your parent is guilty. To do this, they may say things about your parent that are hard for you to hear. They will try to convince the jury that your parent is a bad person, perhaps even dangerous. They try to prove that your parent did in fact commit the crime and should be punished for it; that your parent is too dangerous to be on the streets and should be locked up to protect society. It is their job to convince the jury "beyond a reasonable doubt." Prosecutors ask for the longest sentence that the law allows. In a sense, if they can convince the jury that the person is guilty and convince the judge to give the person a long sentence, they win the case. That is their job.

The Defense

On the other side, your parent's lawyer, called the defense attorney, is trying to convince the jury that your parent is innocent, that he or she did not commit the crime. Our laws say that the defense only has to show that there is a reasonable doubt that your parent committed the crime. If the jury has a reasonable doubt, if they are not sure, they must find the defendant (your parent) not guilty. If your parent is found guilty, it is then the defense's job to persuade the judge to give as short a sentence as possible. If they convince the jury that your parent is not guilty, your parent is acquitted and the defense wins.

Of course, it is really your parent who wins or loses, but in court circles it is often viewed that it is the prosecutor or the defense attorney who wins the case. These two attorneys are in a kind of competition. They each have a job to do, and they each want to win the case. It is the defense attorney's job to provide your parent with the best possible defense, whether he or she personally believes that your parent is guilty or innocent. The opposite is true for the prosecution. It is their job to prosecute your parent even if they personally believe he or she is innocent. In that sense, they are protecting society.

Because no one can know for sure what happened unless they were there, and because people often make decisions based on their emotions, prosecutors often use strong terms in trying to convince the judge or jury. They may exaggerate. If they believe someone might have done something, they will talk as if they know for sure.

Both attorneys try to be convincing; they talk as if they have no doubts, as if they know for sure what they couldn't possible know. As a result, you could hear awful things about your parent. You might learn things about your parent that you never knew, or you might hear things that simply are not true. But whether true or not, whether you believe it or not, it still may be very difficult to hear.

For this reason, parents often do not want their children in court. Even so, they may ask you to come because the defense attorney thinks it might help the case if the jury sees you and your family. It might make the jury more sympathetic to your parent. Or you might be asked to come only at the time of sentencing, in hope that the judge might hand down a lighter sentence.

Whatever happens, going to court can be very difficult, and you should be prepared to be upset. You might need the help of a counselor or therapist before you go into the courtroom, to help you understand what is happening and what you are feeling. Your parents may realize this and get help for you. If you are old enough, you might ask to see a counselor. Even if you feel strong enough not to need emotional support, if may be much easier if you have someone to talk to, at least someone who can explain anything that you don't understand.

PLEA BARGAINING

If the prosecution does not have enough evidence to convict a person or if the evidence strongly points to innocence, they often drop the case and release the person.

If the prosecution think their case is not too strong, they may try to get your parent to plead guilty in exchange for a lighter sentence. This is often a difficult decision for a defendant to make because of what is at stake.

For example, the prosecutor may tell your parent's lawyer that he is willing to recommend to the judge that the sentence be only probation or one year if your parent pleads guilty. If your parent refuses and then loses the case at trial, the sentence will be much longer.

Suppose the prosecutor offers a defendant five to seven years for a plea of guilty, but if the case goes to trial and the defendant is convicted, the sentence may be fifteen years to life. In such cases even innocent people may plead guilty because they are afraid to risk losing the case and doing fifteen years to life. They might decide that they can't take the risk of being away from their family for that long and might accept the five years. This is partly because one can never tell what will happen in court. Even when someone knows he is innocent and has what seems like a good case, something unexpected can happen in court and the innocent person can be found guilty.

NOT KNOWING IS DIFFICULT

Not knowing what is going to happen can be the most difficult thing of all. Sometimes even bad news can be easier to adjust to than uncertainty. Have you ever waited for your report card, not knowing what your grades would be? That waiting time can be very stressful. Even if you finally find out that you failed a course, it may be less stressful than not knowing. Once you know the bad news, you can begin to cope with it. You can direct your energies toward deciding what to do about it. You can plan to attend summer school, or think about how you can bring up the grade next semester. In general, you begin to adapt and adjust to the news.

The same is true when defendants are convicted of a crime. They can begin to think about whether to appeal the sentence. If they accept the sentence, they can begin making some decisions: What arrangements can they make for their family? What will they do in prison? What programs will they participate in? They begin thinking about what they will do when they get out. They have a date in mind when they think they will be released, and they can begin planning for it.

In the same way, the family can begin making plans for getting along without the parent. They now have some idea how long that will be. Their energy begins to have some direction.

Before you know what is going to happen, it is very difficult to make any plans or decisions. All your energy is used up in worrying. This is a time when everyone feels helpless. There is nothing to do but wait. Often there is nothing you can do until you know what will happen. There is no way you can affect what will happen in court. You have no way of knowing what the jury will decide, or what the judge and lawyers are going to do. You may not even know what your parent is going to do. Often *he* does not know what he will do; he may be feeling as helpless as you. It can be very hurtful to see your parent helpless or frightened. Your parent always seemed to be in charge, to know what to do. Now no one knows what to do, because no one knows what is going to happen.

So you can see that the time in jail, before being convicted or released, can often be the most difficult time for everyone.

HOW TO COPE WITH PUBLICITY

One of the most difficult things to cope with when a parent is arrested may be the publicity surrounding the case. You may see stories about your parent in newspapers or on television. You may hear the story on the radio. Your friends, teachers, and other people may hear about the case, and all of a sudden you may find yourself the center of attention.

Kids who don't know any better may make fun of you or tease you. People may say hurtful things about you or your parent. Some people say things without thinking, or talk without knowing the facts. Some people like to take advantage of a situation to feel important. Teasing or making fun of other people makes them feel big. Sometimes people use put-downs because they are afraid. They fear anyone or anything that they do not understand, so they are irrationally afraid of anyone remotely connected with a crime, especially a violent crime. People often believe in stereotypes (false assumptions about groups of people). Some of the stereotypes that may affect you are, "The fruit doesn't fall far from the tree," or "Like father, like son," or "bad blood."

Your Personality

Such sayings stem from fear and ignorance. Many factors contribute to a your personality and the way you behave. Only one of those factors has to do with what you learn from your parents. Others are the special strengths and talents you are born with; how hard you work to develop those skills; the people who have had influence on your life, such as your other parent, relatives, teachers, and friends; the choices you make in your life, and any special help you might receive such as counseling or therapy. You may choose to be like your parent in some ways and not in others. No one needs to be a replica of their parents. You can adopt those qualities of your parents that you like, that help you get along well in life, and ignore those that you do not like or do not work well in your life. Each person is unique. It is very important not to accept other people's opinion of you, especially when that opinion has nothing to do with who you are but rather with a generalization that has nothing to do with you.

The publicity about your parent's case may be very different from what you know the situation to be. Remember that the media sensationalize; they report events in an exaggerated way to catch the attention of their audience, and at times that is more important to them than the truth. The media want to sell advertising in their newspaper, on their TV channel, or on their radio station. As a result, they focus on any exceptional or unusual event.

The time while your parent is in the news will be very difficult for you and your family. You may become a center of attention. Try to remember that other events will soon be in the news, and people will forget your story. It may seem that it will never end, but there is not much you can do but wait.

CHAPTER ◇ 6

Prison

Prisons come in many shapes and sizes, and although they have some things in common, they also have many differences. The most familiar type of correctional institution is the large, fortresslike, maximum-security prison. Such structures as San Quentin prison in California are characterized by their massive size, thick stone walls, gun towers, steel doors, multitiered cell blocks, large populations, and rural locations. Medium- and minimum-security prisons are more open and have less strict security procedures. Minimum-security prisons are sometimes called camps; they look more like a military camp than a prison, without barbed-wired fences or other barriers. Prisoners in these facilities may be on work release, home furlough, or other programs under which they can leave the prison for limited periods and in general are less confined.

Besides work programs, many prisons have a wide range of medical, counseling, and other rehabilitation services. These may include schools, GED programs, college degree programs, and various shops such as auto mechanics, woodworking, or electronics. When inmates are allowed to work, they are paid minimum wages.

It must be emphasized, however, that prisons are not schools, factories, hospitals, or psychiatric centers. First and foremost, they are places of confinement. The increasing size of the prison population almost guarantees that, in the future, most prisons will serve primarily as holding facilities, not as places of rehabilitation.

GROWTH OF PRISONS

Until the 18th century, prisons were not the principal way society dealt with citizens who broke laws. Criminals were exiled, executed, or suffered various forms of corporal punishment. Although jails were common, imprisonment was viewed as a temporary restriction rather than the prescribed penalty for crime. Prisons ranged from workhouses for those who were in debt (Bridewell in Great Britain and the Maison de Force in Belgium) to institutions such as the Hospice of San Michel in Rome, which was primarily designed to incarcerate incorrigible boys. During the period called the "Enlightenment," the extreme harshness of most punishment was questioned for the first time. Society began trying to fit the severity of the punishment to the severity of the crime, in the belief that clear and just penalties would act as a deterrent to crime. These underlying beliefs of European society have carried over to the United States. Many believe, however, that the basic assumptions of this type of system are flawed and therefore do not work. Others believe that the system has become so prejudiced and corrupt that it mostly functions to control certain categories of people by locking them up rather than really attempting to improve society.

PRISON

Whatever the facts, today a prison is a facility maintained for the confinement of convicted felons. Felonies are serious crimes punishable by a year or more in prison, as opposed to misdemeanors, which are less serious crimes punishable by fines, community service, or in some cases less than a year in jail.

In the past decade the prison population has grown faster than it had since prisons began. Most of this has been related to the war on drugs and the increase in drug problems and poverty in our country. As a result, the prisons have become more and more overcrowded and therefore more dangerous and more difficult for prisoners and prison guards alike.

Many things that have been said about jail are also true of prisons, although there are some major differences. Among the things that are the same is the major purpose of jails and prisons—to incarcerate people who have committed a crime. They have broken a law or a number of laws to the extent that society has determined that they need punishment or that they represent a risk to the public, or both. Therefore they must be removed from the mainstream of society and kept where where they cannot continue to violate the law or be a danger to others.

DETERRENCE

Another belief held by many in our society is that imprisonment acts as a deterrent to crime; that is, the fear of going to prison will cause people to avoid criminal behavior. Those who hold this view also often believe that the harsher or longer the sentence, the greater the deterrent to crime. This view is controversial, and many experts in criminal law and justice do not agree with it. They point to the fact that in states that have adopted longer or harsher sentences, the crime rate has not significantly decreased. In fact, in many instances where stiffer penalties are enacted, crime rates go up. Two examples of this argument are the laws against drugs and the death penalty. As was discussed in Chapter 1, as longer sentences were mandated for drug offenses, there was no decline in the number of arrests for drug crimes or drug-related crimes. In fact, the stricter the laws became, the more people were arrested. In the same vein, statistics show that the death penalty for murder does not result in a decrease in murders committed; that is, as states instituted the death penalty, there was no decrease in the number of murders committed in those states.

The Opposite View

According to a 1992 article by Dennis Cauchon in USA Today, a Sentencing Commission study found that long sentences appear to have no significant impact on recidivism. "A high incarceration rate does not lower the crime rate," says University of Arizona criminologist Mark Gottfredson. "If it did, we would have seen some evidence by now." In the same article, Joseph Lehman, then Pennsylvania Corrections Commissioner, said, "Today, we use prisons as the solution for everything—it doesn't work." The same paper reported that whereas in 1980 one of every 362 adults was in prison or jail, in 1992 the figure was one of every 156 adults. It forecast that in 2000 one of every 99 adults will live in a cell. In 1991 there were 1,248,011 people in prison and jail in this country.

You might ask, if stiffer and stricter sentences have not decreased the crime rate, why do we keep trying something that does not work? The answer is not simple. Probably a lot of it has to do with people's prejudices and fears. When people are afraid, they try to protect themselves in any way they can, even if the way they choose doesn't always make sense. People often fear what they don't understand. Emotions, prejudices, and their preconceived notions do not always give way to reason or even common sense.

Other people believe strongly that the way to combat crime—to reduce the need for people to commit crimes—is to reduce poverty, to give people decent homes and the ability to support themselves and their families. Day care for working mothers, affordable health care, prenatal and early infant care are but a few alternatives that many people stress as preferable to harsher sentences and more prisons. The people who propose these ways of fighting crime point to the fact that it costs less to send a person to college for four years than to keep him in jail for the same time. This segment of society believes in preventing problems before they arise rather than trying to fix them afterward or punish people for what they may have felt forced to do. It is true that most people are not really forced to commit crime; however, many people do not have an equal opportunity to earn honest money.

THE SYSTEM OF JUSTICE

When you think about prisons, remember that they are part of a larger system—our system of justice and laws. People can be sent to prison only if society believes they have broken a law, but laws are made by governments and they can be changed by governments. What is law today may not be law tomorrow.

For example, when abortion was illegal, a woman could be sent to prison for having an abortion, and a doctor could be sent to prison for performing an abortion. When the law changed, the same woman or doctor could not be sent to prison. In some states certain sexual acts are illegal. In many states it is still against the law for adult homosexual men to have sex with each other, even if both agree and it is done in the privacy of their home. It is illegal to have sex with persons under a certain age. In some states it is even illegal for married persons to have certain kinds of sex in the privacy of their home. Married adults do not usually go to jail for having sex, but it is an example of laws that society establishes but does not enforce.

NONVIOLENT CRIME

Failure to pay taxes is against the law and can send people to prison. For a medical person or other professional to fail to report child abuse can send them to prison. Refusing to testify in court under certain circumstances can send a person to jail; it is called being in contempt of court. For example, if a counselor is ordered to testify about what a client said in counseling, and he or she refuses to do so, it could mean jail. Lying under oath (perjury) is illegal and can result in imprisonment. These are a few of many so-called nonviolent crimes that can send one to jail. In general, people who break a law whether or not they know they are breaking a law can be arrested and sent to jail or prison. Some people go to jail rather than compromise their beliefs; for example, in the 1960s men went to jail rather than serve in the Vietnam War because they believed the war was wrong.

What this makes clear is that not everyone in prison is there for a violent offense. Not everyone in prison has even done things that most of us would consider "bad." Also, not everyone in prison is poor, although most are.

Some are successful businessmen who were cheating on their taxes or making money in illegal ways. This is called white-collar crime, since it is often committed by people who wear shirts and ties to work.

Nevertheless, it is our current system of laws and punishments that you will have to cope with if your parent goes to prison. In addition, you may be forced to cope with the prejudices, generalizations, and misperceptions of many people who do not understand what prison is like, or what people in prison are like. It is important for you to learn what is real and what is not, to begin to separate fact from fiction. This book covers some of the facts but certainly could not discuss all of them. Also, the information is subject to change.

People in prison often refer to it as being "behind the wall," meaning walls that often surround prisons to keep the prisoners in and in some ways the outside world out. The men and women behind those walls develop a way of living with each other, of getting by in the confines of incarcerated life. In some ways it is like life outside, but in other ways very different. In part because of the isolation of prison life, inmates often develop a culture quite different from that of the outside world.

PRISON VERSUS JAIL

As mentioned before, people are held in jail while they are awaiting trial. If sentenced to more than one year, they are normally transferred to the appropriate prison in their state. That means that prisoners have a fairly good idea of how long they will be there. If they are sentenced to five to ten years, they know that it will be a minimum of five years before they are eligible to apply to the Parole Board for release. There are, of course, exceptions; for example, if someone wins an appeal or receives a pardon. In most situations, however, prisoners serve at least the minimum length of their sentence. The more often they have been arrested, especially for felonies, and the more serious the crime, of course, the longer they are likely to remain in prison.

Programs

Because most people remain in prison much longer than in jails, prisoners are much more likely to get to know one another and to depend on each other for help and companionship. In addition, more programs are available to occupy time and to help prepare them for release. Most prisoners participate in one program or another; some participate in many. Examples include work programs, school programs, counseling programs, trade programs, and others. Prisoners may attend classes during the day and work in the laundry room at night. Some take full advantage of educational programs. Prisoners who never finished high school may leave prison after several years with a college degree.

As a result, many inmates who have served several years in prison say that the time was much easier and went much faster than even a few months in jail. In addition, prisons can be much safer and calmer than jails because the inmates have their energies directed in different ways. The population is more stable, and people form relationships and settle into a more predictable and stable way of living.

Another factor that makes prisons sometimes safer than jails is that the prisoners' record counts toward the release date. If they break the rules, they get a "ticket," which results in punishment.

Punishment

Normal punishment is a further restriction of freedom. For example, they may have to spend time in solitary confinement, a cell in a special cell block where prisoners are locked in twenty-four hours a day, given their meals in the cell, and allowed out only occasionally for a shower or a walk. In some facilities prisoners in solitary are allowed out once a week, sometimes more often, sometimes less. In some prisons solitary confinement is called the "hole," because it is an empty cell, sometimes without light or even a bed to sleep on. If prisoners are suicidal or have other problems, they themselves may be stripped so that there is nothing they can hang themselves with. The time in solitary depends on the offense and how often the prisoner has committed offenses. Attacking an officer usually results in many months in the hole.

Relationships

Of course, prison always creates the tensions of large numbers of men living together, needing to find ways of relating to each other, needing to protect themselves and at times each other. With all of this comes the need for dominance over others and the constant need not to appear weak. Prisoners sometimes get involved in fights simply to prove that they can, encouraging others to leave them alone. At the same time, because getting into trouble can affect their "good time" (early release), there is an opposing motivation not to get into trouble. Many prisoners live by the principle of keeping to themselves, minding their own business and staying "clean," out of trouble.

The same principles of secrecy apply in prison as in jail.

Secrecy is a large part of the prison culture. Inmates do not tell on other inmates, nor do they tell on officers. That adds to the danger, in that one feels things can happen that no one will ever hear about. Some prisoners say that although violence is less constant in prison than in jail, when conflict occurs, it is more serious. However, most prisoners serve their time without being killed or seriously hurt. They mind their business, keep to themselves, and do what they have to do to get by.

JOE'S FATHER

At seventeen years of age, Joe was hoping to be with his father for the first birthday in ten years. His mother had died when he was a baby. His father, Greg, was serving seven to twelve years for possession of a gun. It seemed like a long sentence for such an offense, but Greg was a "predicate": He had prior felony convictions and had been on parole when he was picked up with a gun. The sad part was that Greg had been working and keeping his nose clean. He wasn't doing drugs, wasn't drinking, didn't hang around with ex-convicts, and was working hard. Joe's father made one big mistake: He got caught while buying a hand gun for protection for his home. Since he was on parole and had prior convictions, he was hit with the maximum sentence. It seemed as if Joe and his father had the worst luck in the world. However, Greg was up for parole next month, and Joe was really hoping that they would let him go this time.

In fact, in some ways Greg seemed to do better in prison that he did outside. He took an auto mechanic course and learned how to repair cars. His prison counselor set him up with someone near Greg's home who was willing to take a chance on an ex-con. The fact that Greg had a job waiting for him, a son, and a home that his brother had been able to keep up would make his chances of parole much better. The Parole Board is reluctant to release anyone unless he has a place to live and a job.

Joe had been lucky. Joe's uncle had moved into his home, made the payments, and taken care of him while his father was in prison. Joe's uncle worked and was able to keep the home going.

Joe's story had a happy outcome. Greg appeared before the Parole Board and was to be released two weeks before Joe's birthday. Although at times it had seemed like an eternity before Joe would be with his father again, now the time flew. In two weeks Joe would again be living with his father. It would be the best birthday gift ever.

CHAPTER ◊ 7

Life After Jail: Parole

P arole is the early release of a prisoner before completion of the sentence. It is a key factor in the indeterminate sentence, a sentence that may turn out to be less than the actual years specified.

When people are sentenced, they are normally eligible for parole some time before the sentence is over. They can return home and serve the rest of the sentence on parole. They usually have to report to a parole officer on a regular basis and follow certain rules.

Not everyone is eligible for parole. It depends on the crime and the person's criminal history. Like probation, release on parole is conditional. If the offender violates the conditions or commits a new crime, the parole can be revoked and the offender returned to prison to complete the sentence. The parole decision is made by a Parole Board, an administrative body of people with a background in criminal justice who have been appointed for a fixed term.

CRITICISM OF PAROLE

Critics of probation and parole contend that such practices are too lenient and permit the offender to escape deserved punishment. Such criticisms have led to laws that forbid probation when offenders are convicted of violent crimes and that limit the use of parole. Other observers believe that if offenders have shown good behavior in prison and a will to reform, they should be entitled to reduction of their actual time in prison. In addition, it is very costly to keep many people in prison, and this is one way of relieving the overcrowding and expense. It also gives offenders something to look forward to and work toward while serving their sentence.

Parole is intended to be a transition back to society. While parolees are no longer in custody, they continue to be provided with some structure and assistance by reporting to their parole officer. A good parole officer provides advice and helps with the adjustments needed to live once more in society.

A CHANGED LIFE

Those adjustments can be many and very difficult. Parolees are used to a way of life in which everything was controlled. They did not need to worry about holding a job or coping with relationships with family and friends. They have not had to act as a father, boyfriend or girlfriend, or husband or wife for some time. It was easier to avoid the temptations of drugs and alcohol because those things were not so readily available.

The parolees may have earned a certain status within the prison, gained respect for their courage, strength, or experience inside the walls. Now they have to start all over again. It may be hard to find means of support. It may be even more difficult to provide emotional support for their family, who will depend on them in a way they are no longer accustomed to. In prison, they had only to take care of themselves. They lived independently. At first that may have been very difficult, but in time they probably grew accustomed to it. Now these patterns again have to change.

In addition, men or women released from prison are often embarrassed about having served time. They may be embarrassed about things that they did while in prison, or things that happened to them. They may be embarrassed about having committed the crime that put them in prison, or having been caught. They return to the world with a criminal record, which may bar them from many types of jobs. They may have lost their license to practice their profession and have to find something completely new to do to earn a living and restore some purpose to their lives. Their self-esteem is often affected in that they think less of themselves and are vulnerable to what others may think of them. All this makes some people depressed, irritable, or frightened. In addition, they may not be able to ask for help or even know that they need help, because they have hidden their fear or other feelings for so long.

SUSAN AND JACK'S FATHER

Susan and Jack's father, Jim Seever, was scheduled to appear before the Parole Board in two weeks. They had visited him in prison the day before and knew that he was very nervous about it. He had applied for parole last year for the first time and had been denied. Although he had been a model prisoner, the Board didn't consider him ready for release.

This was Jim Seever's second sentence on a felony conviction. He had a bad temper and once before had been arrested for assault after a drunken fight in a bar.

This time he had been arrested for assault and robbery. Again drinking in a bar, he had gotten into a fight with a man who owed him money. The man had owed the debt for several months but always had an excuse for not paying. Now Jim needed the money to pay a gambling debt of his own.

Jim knew that he couldn't afford to get into any more trouble. He was still on parole, under the terms of which he was not allowed to drink or to be out after midnight. His parole officer knew that Jim was an alcoholic and had set these conditions purposely to keep him out of trouble.

But when the man again started making excuses for not paying, the liquor got the better of Jim, and he knocked the man to the ground. Not content with that, he reached into the man's pocket for his wallet, intending to take the money he was owed. At that point the man screamed for help, a police officer appeared, and Jim Seever was arrested.

Because of his prior felony conviction and because he was on parole, Jim was sentenced to two to four years on top of the three years that remained of his previous term. That meant another seven years, but he would be eligible for parole again in four years.

Finally realizing that he had a problem, Jim Seever participated in many prison programs. He attended counseling sessions and went regularly to meetings of Alcoholics Anonymous. He also worked and attended college courses. He got along very well with his counselor, who recommended that he be released on parole. They had talked for several years about how he would do things differently this time. He would continue with Alcoholics

Anonymous, get a sponsor, and continue counseling with a drug counselor.

This plan had worked well when Jim Seever had been released the first time. He had managed to keep out of trouble for two years. His family were very proud of him, and Susan and Jack were especially happy to have a father again. He had gotten a job in construction and was making good money. The family rented a new home in the suburbs, and Susan and Jack were just beginning to forget about their father's prison days when they realized that he had begun drinking again.

It seemed that their parents were having more and more marital problems. Like many men who have been in prison, Jim Seever had trouble maintaining a close relationship with his wife. Closeness and intimacy frightened him, and his way of keeping a distance between them was to fight with her. She in turn was still angry with him for having gotten arrested the first time, and she lived in fear of his going to prison again.

Unfortunately, the Seevers did not seek marriage or family counseling. The fighting increased, and one night Jack and Susan overheard their mother threaten to divorce her husband.

Under the pressure at home, Jim started missing AA meetings and began to drink instead. The drinking increased rapidly, and Susan and Jack were sure it was only a question of time before their father was in trouble again, but they felt helpless. And sure enough, he broke his parole, beat up the man who owed him money, and was back in prison.

This time, however, Mrs. Seever took a different course. She was worried because Susan seemed depressed most of the time and Jack was beginning to have trouble in school. So she and her children made a visit to a family counseling center. At first they all blamed themselves, but the family therapist was able to help them see that the entire family was suffering in one way or another because of Jim Seever's imprisonment. Each member of the family felt in some way responsible for Jim's mistakes and was worried about how they would be able to get along as a family without him. As time passed they also worried how they would get along *with* him when he was again released. Although they missed Jim very much, they had gotten used to life without him. They all dreaded having the fighting start again.

And yet they all felt guilty about these thoughts, and each one thought he or she was the only one thinking that way. None of them could admit not wanting their father to come home because they couldn't stand the idea of the fighting. Nor could they bear to get their hopes up, only to have them dashed a second time.

When the therapist suggested that they might all have mixed feelings about having the head of the family come home, Jack was shocked to hear his mother and sister admit having the same thoughts that he was struggling with. Each of them was afraid the others would think him or her bad for having such thoughts. How could you not want your father to come home?

What the therapist also helped them learn was that people rarely want only one thing. People often want and don't want the same thing at the same time. The human mind is often in conflict with itself. It has competing wishes and fears.

For example, how often have you been asked what flavor of ice cream you want and have had to think about it because you want two flavors equally. To take it a little further, you might want to do your homework because you want a good grade in school and you want to please your parents, but you also want to go out and play because it is fun and you want to please your friends. You want to do both things at the same time, and you have to decide which one is more important. Or you might want to try a ride at the amusement park because it seems exciting and fun, but you also are more than a little scared.

Likewise in the Seever family all wanted their father home because they loved him and missed him and they wanted a father whom they could depend on and who would do things with them and for them. At the same time, they wanted peace at home, and they were afraid that if he came home the fighting would start again. They wanted both things at the same time.

The therapist helped them realize that this was not bad; it was simply a human response. It was the way our minds work. Ambivalence is a part of almost every decision we make. Once the Seevers began to realize this, they felt less isolated with their thoughts and less guilty. Susan was less depressed and began to express herself more clearly, first in the counseling sessions and then at home. Jack felt less distracted in school; because he could accept his thoughts better, he began to concentrate better in school and improve his grades.

The therapist urged them to continue the family therapy after Mr. Seever returned home so that they could work out problems as they arose and get support from the therapist and from each other to express their thoughts to their father. It was important that he realize what they were going through as well.

When the great day came and the Parole Board released Jim, all four Seevers were much better prepared to face life together. It was hard to tell Jim that they wanted him to go to family therapy with them, but with the therapist's support they were able to do so, and he agreed. They were astonished, but because of the counseling he had received in prison, he now thought more highly of therapy and was willing to do this with them. He was also worried about doing all the right things when he was released this time. He realized that he had failed in his first parole, and he was as concerned as his wife and children that the same thing not happen again. He never wanted to leave his family again.

PAROLE CAN BE DIFFICULT

It is never easy for adults to be told what they can and cannot do. It is also not easy for people to be told that they have problems and need help. When convicts are placed on parole, they are given many rules that they must follow or risk having their parole revoked and going back to prison to serve the rest of their term.

Rules of Parole

Some parole rules depend on the crime; for example, a man convicted of child molesting may not go where children congregate, as in a schoolyard or playground. Other rules are the same for everyone. No one on parole may be seen drinking alcohol or, of course, using illegal drugs. They may have a curfew, a time when they must be at home. They have to report whenever they move or change jobs. They have to report if they lose a job and what efforts they are making to find another. They may not associate with anyone with a criminal history or anyone they knew in prison. Of course, they are not allowed to carry a weapon of any kind. They have to report regularly to their parole officer. That may start with once a week and change to every other week or once a month, depending on how they are doing.

The parole officer may make surprise visits to their home to check whether they are following all of the rules. It is not easy for grown men or women to have someone checking up on them. It can be embarrassing to parents for their children to know that they have rules to follow or must report to a parole officer. They are used to being in a position of authority with their children. They may feel less of a man or a woman because they have been in prison.

Family Conflicts

Family members also may have many conflicts when one of them is on parole, especially if that member is a parent. Children may be very disturbed if they learn that their parent is violating parole and taking the risk of returning to jail. They may or may not be able to talk to their parents about these worries. Many parents are already upset about risking being sent back to prison because of what they are doing, but they may feel unable to control themselves. Because they are so upset and feel so vulnerable, they may explode at their children for bringing up the topic. They may resent criticism from their children. In fact, they are really angry at themselves for taking risks, but they may take out that anger on a child or anyone close by.

Seeking Help

The most difficult part, is that the child or teenager who sees this happening may be powerless to do anything about it. Teenagers especially have a hard enough time keeping themselves and doing what they are supposed to do without having to worry about what their parents are doing. They have no power to change their parents' behavior, so there is really little they can do except worry. If they have the courage, they can seek another adult to help them with these concerns. Often teenagers are afraid to tell anyone about such worries; it feels like telling on their parent and perhaps getting their parents sent back to jail.

You should know that if you seek counseling from any licensed professional, that person is required to keep confidential anything you say in a counseling session. That means that he or she cannot tell anyone what you say without your permission.

There are a few exceptions to this rule. If you tell a counselor that you want to kill yourself or kill someone else, and if the counselor believes that the danger is real, he or she is obligated to take whatever steps are necessary to protect you or the other person from harm. Counselors and therapists will notify a parent or guardian and if necessary hospitalize anyone who is suicidal or homicidal. In addition, if you report to a professional that you or another child is being physically abused, the counselor is required to notify protective services and take steps to protect you or the other child.

With those few exceptions, anything that you talk to a counselor about remains confidential unless you want that information shared with someone else. A counselor should not report to anyone that your parent is violating probation unless that parent is directly abusing you or another child. The counselor's job is to help you decide what to do. At times there is nothing you can do, and the counselor's job becomes simply helping you accept that and cope with the anxieties and fears you are suffering.

Remember that childhood and adolescence are difficult times for you, and you need some adult or counselor that you trust to help you understand and cope with all that is happening to you and inside of you. Your future happiness and success depend on your ability to cope with these things in your early years so that you have the energy and the ability to prepare yourself for the future. And it is very important to remember that you deserve a good future. You deserve every opportunity to make the most of your life, and you can't do that if you are overwhelmed with problems and worries about that is happening to your parents. When you are an adult, it will be your turn to help other youngsters handle the many problems of growing up. Right now it is your turn to ask for help and to receive it, so that some day you will be able to pass it on to others.

CHAPTER ◇ 8

What Does All This Mean About Me?

We have talked a lot about the legal system, courts, probation, parole, prisons, and jails. And we have talked about your parents and what they may be going through. But perhaps the most important topic is how all this affects you. You can't change the system or your parents, but you can do something about the impact on you. Probably the most important aspect of having a parent in jail is how it affects the way you think and feel about yourself. How does it affect your relationships with your parents, siblings, and relatives, your friends and teachers, but most of all, your relationship with yourself.

What does it mean to have a relationship with one's self? We are much more used to thinking about how we relate to others, how we think about them and act toward them. We know what it means to be harsh and mean to others, or kind and understanding. But how often do we consider how we treat ourselves? This chapter addresses that issue along with what having a parent in jail might mean about you and what it does not mean about you.

LIKE AND UNLIKE

We have all heard the expression "like father, like son," meaning that often we become like our parents in many ways. After all, they are the first persons we know in this world. They are the ones who care for us and teach us how to talk, walk, dress, be with others. They socialize us and teach us right from wrong. They are the first to teach us that we can't go around hitting or biting others, that we don't take what is not ours, how and where to go to the bathroom, how to clean ourselves, shower, brush our teeth. They teach us how to address others, when to say please and thank you, how to share, and how to behave in numerous situations. They also teach us to protect ourselves and value ourselves by telling us what is dangerous and what we should not do.

They often teach us how we should feel about ourselves. The way our parents feel about us has a lot to do with how we feel about ourselves. If they love and value us, we feel lovable and valuable. Of course, if they did not feel that way about themselves, it may be hard for them to express those feelings toward us. When we don't get these good things from our parents, we may have problems with our self-esteem. We may feel unlovable or not worth much. The truth is that everyone is valuable and everyone is lovable, but we may not all realize that.

Ways of Learning

One of the most important things parents can teach us is how to protect ourselves. They teach us not to cross the street without looking, or not to touch a hot stove or play with matches. They teach us how to ask for what we want and stand up for ourselves, and also when it is more important to share or wait our turn. If everything goes well, we learn all the rules, and we are "socialized" in the particular society to which we belong. Often parents teach us by example. By watching what they do, we learn. When we see our parents sitting at the table and using silverware and a napkin, we learn to do the same. However, we gradually learn that not everything our parents do is the best thing. No one is perfect, not even our parents.

As we go to school and learn from other people, we realize that our parents are fallible. We learn that others see things differently. This is often not an easy time for young people, as they feel a conflict between what they learned from their parents and what they hear from others, which may not be the same thing. At that time we begin to make choices: I will be like my parents in this way but not that way. I like this about my parents and don't like that about them. I agree with my parents on this topic but not that topic. For example, we may have heard our parents talk about other nationalities or races in a way that seems to us prejudiced and not fair, so we may not agree with their prejudices but still agree with them on other things. It is important to remember that no one is ever completely right or completely wrong. Very few things in life are completely one way or the other.

Uniqueness

We may look a little like one or both of our parents but dress very differently. We may have some of the talents they have and other talents they do not have. We may grow up like them in some ways but not in other ways. The point is that no one is ever just like their father or just like their mother. We are like our parents in some ways and not in other ways. It is true that we have learned many of our beliefs, our values from them, but we have also learned many things from other people such as teachers, relatives, friends, perhaps a clergyperson. Most people are a combination of all of their experiences in life, taking aspects of every experience to make up a unique and special identity. In addition, there is a part of us that will learn and accept certain things we are taught and reject other things. Some of us have easygoing, calm personalities and can be quiet, learn more easily, and get along with many people. Others are more active, aggressive, excitable, and take longer to learn certain things. Because of our biological makeup, some of us learn more easily by listening, others by doing. Some of us may be good with our hands, while others are better with words and concepts. We may be better at math than reading, or visa versa. Because we are a combination of our mother, our father, everyone else who has had an influence on us, and of ourselves, we are not exactly like anyone else. We are unique. This sometimes makes things difficult, but it also makes us special—special simply because no one else is exactly like us and no one else ever will be. Realizing and understanding this is what helps us to have a healthy self-esteem, to feel good about ourselves simply because we are who we are.

Self-Esteem

Often we have a false sense of self-esteem, based on what others think of us, or what we have, or what we can do. The only kind of self-esteem that is healthy and helps us continue to feel good about ourselves is the type that comes from what *we think* and can appreciate about ourselves. It's what *you* think about your parent's imprisonment that is important.

You probably have mixed emotions about a parent who is in jail. Some kids are angry that their parent did what he or she did. Others are angry at the police or the courts for having sent their parent to jail. You may be disappointed in your parent, especially if this is not the first arrest and if your parent promised it would not happen again. It is likely that you are frightened about what might happen to your family if it is your father who is in jail. You might be worried about yourself and what will happen to you without your father at home.

Feelings

You might even be relieved that your parent is no longer at home if you have been abused or things have been difficult and frightening at home. If you do feel relieved, you might also feel guilty about those feelings, even though one cannot help one's feelings. It is important to remember that feelings are neither right nor wrong; they simply exist. It is perfectly natural to feel relieved if your parent was abusive.

You might also be relieved to have the parent arrested because otherwise he or she might have been hurt worse or have hurt someone else. This is especially true when drugs are involved. Often people in jail say that if they had not been arrested they would have died or been killed while on drugs; they were out of control.

You may feel guilty or upset with yourself. Often kids think they could have done something to help their parent or prevent their parent from being arrested. This is almost never the case. There is seldom anything anyone can do to stop someone from doing things that are wrong or that will hurt them. If you are having certain feelings, you can be sure that many other kids in your position have had the same feelings. You can be sure that your feelings are normal and not wrong. The only thing wrong would be to blame yourself for having feelings that you could not prevent.

Blaming Yourself

You may also be having strange thoughts. You may think something is wrong with you because there must be something wrong with your parent. The fact is that all of us make mistakes and at times do things we shouldn't do. There may be something wrong with your parent, but then there is something wrong with almost everyone. No one is perfect, not even parents. There may even be things wrong with you, things that you need help with or could do differently or better. However, the fact that your parent has done something wrong does not mean that there is anything like that wrong with you.

Remember, as we said earlier, everyone is like their parents in some ways and different from them in many other ways. No one is a carbon copy of anyone else. Everyone is unique. Sometimes people in the same family are as different as day and night. You may think that because one or both of your parents have gone to jail, you will end up there also. You might even have heard people say such stupid things. The fact is that nothing about parents' going to jail can make their child do the same thing. You have the opportunity to be different. You can follow in your parents' footsteps in the good ways, not the bad ways. In fact, you may even learn from their mistakes and not have to make those mistakes yourself. What happens to you will be a result of the choices you make, and you must always remember that you have many choices.

Talk Is Cheap

If your parent is in jail, people will say lots of things. Some of the things people say are smart, some are very stupid. If you believed everything you heard, you would be in a lot of trouble. Your opinion would depend on who was talking to you, and they might be right or they might be very wrong. Suppose one person tells you that you are from "bad seed" and the fact that your parent is in prison means that you are no good either. Then another person tells you that you really are a good person and that your parent's going to jail has nothing to do with your being good or bad. Which one do you believe?

Too often people's feelings about themselves depend on the last thing that they have heard. When they hear good things about themselves, they feel good; their self-esteem is high. When they hear bad things about themselves, they feel bad, and their self-esteem falls. One's self-esteem cannot depend on the last person you talk to. To be healthy, it has to be stable, self-contained. It must come from your opinion of yourself regardless of what others say or think. If two people have opposite opinions of you, it is still you they are talking about. You haven't changed; only their opinions are different. Which one should you believe?

Your self-esteem has to come from who you are, not always what you do or what happens to you. After all, people sometimes do things well and sometimes not so well. We can't always succeed. If scientists gave up every time an experiment failed, they would never discover anything. To succeed, they have to try hundreds of experiments that do not work. Each one that doesn't work teaches them something new, and next time they know what not to do. Eventually, if they keep at it, one experiment works and they have discovered something new.

Changing Roles

Other strange thoughts that kids sometimes have when a parent goes to jail is that they should now be the man or the woman of the house. They think they have to take over the role of father or mother, of caring for their family. No matter how much you might want to, you can't grow up overnight. Grown-ups sometimes forget that and expect more from children than they should.

You cannot be the man or the woman of the house because you are the age that you are. Because you are not yet adult, you need and deserve adults around to help you out.

Perhaps someone told you that you have to take charge. People often say such silly things because they are not thinking clearly. How can you be something that you are not? Especially when there is a crisis, adults don't always think straight. That is why it is important that people ask for help when they need it. When someone is arrested or imprisoned, everyone in that person's family, or even people who know that person, may be in crisis. They may be confused and not be thinking clearly. That is why it is important to seek counseling at such times.

Professionals can help people think more clearly and can help the family plan for surviving this crisis with as little hardship as possible. If there is anything good about crisis, it is that it is a time when things change. Whenever things change, there is the chance that they may change for the better.

It may be hard to believe, but a parent's imprisonment may be an opportunity, with the right help, to change many things for the better. The family members may grow closer. They may learn more about themselves and about each other and be able to pull together and help each other in a new way. People being what they are, they do not do much to change things unless they have to. No one likes change. We often want things to stay the way they are because it feels safer, even if the reality is that it is not safer.

BOB'S EXPERIENCE

Bob was only sixteen when his father was arrested for the first time. It was the beginning of the summer, and Bob was looking forward to vacation after a hard junior year in high school. As far as Bob knew, his father, Paul Blanchard, never did anything wrong. He went to work every day, came home every night, and spent time with his family. Paul was an account executive in a large corporation, and Bob's mother, Lillian, was a legal secretary who often worked long hours. They lived well and had a nice home in the suburbs.

One day something happened that stunned Bob. His father was arrested for embezzlement. It seemed that Paul had accumulated a lot of bills. The Blanchards were living beyond their means, and Paul was having trouble meeting payments on all of the things they had purchased: the new house, the boat, the summer place. One day it occurred to him that he could skim a little money off the top of the books without anyone's missing it. It was too easy, and as time went on he took more and more until one day someone became suspicious and the company began an investigation. Paul was arrested at home, late one night. The family spent a month in and out of court until Paul decided to plead guilty. The district attorney offered him three to six years in federal prison, which he accepted. With good behavior, Paul could be paroled in three years.

In the meantime, what were Bob and his mother to do? They still had all the bills, and Lillian's salary was limited. Bob had had a good junior year, and he had hoped to go to college the year after next. Now it seemed that all his plans would have to change. How could he think of going away while his father was in prison, and how would he help his mother with her new responsibilities? He didn't know where to turn. His mother was too upset to talk, and he was embarrassed to tell any of his friends, although he figured they would soon find out. He thought about talking to the school counselor but was afraid.

As it turned out, one of his teachers did find out and asked Bob to stay after class to talk. The teacher assured Bob that he had nothing to be ashamed of and asked him to think about seeing the school social worker. The teacher said he knew of other kids in school whose parents were in jail and that the social worker had been able to help some of them. Bob was astonished to hear of other parents going to jail, but he took the teacher's advice and met with the social worker. After getting to know Bob, Mrs. Prince suggested that she call Bob's mother and arrange for the three of them to meet. Bob agreed.

That was the best thing Bob ever did. Mrs. Prince helped his mother with concrete suggestions to make the crisis have as little adverse affect on the family as possible. With the aid of a lawyer, Lillian was able to arrange for payment of the debts in a way that she could better afford. It would take a long time to pay them off, but at least the family would be able to survive. Over the next year, there were many difficult adjustments to make. With the ongoing help of Mrs. Prince and others, Lillian sold their expensive house, the summer place, and the boat. With the money she saved, she was able to continue payments of the loans as well as make arrangements for Bob's college. Mrs. Prince helped Bob apply to city colleges, and because of his grades he was able to go to a school that offered the communication courses he wanted to take.

Things weren't easy, but they weren't as bad as Bob had first expected. Mrs. Prince helped to define things at home so that Bob did not feel obliged to be the man of the house but was able to continue being a teenager and a student. Life was not the same, but Bob learned lessons about taking care of himself, cooperation, saving, and other things that he might never have learned if his father had continued to buy things with money that wasn't theirs.

In addition, it was very important for Bob to be able to talk with the counselor when people said things that hurt him or that simply weren't true. He needed the support of someone who knew how to listen to teenagers and who could help him anticipate things that he never expected.

For example, an insensitive teacher one day got mad at Bob and blurted out in front of the whole class that Bob would never amount to anything, that he would turn out exactly like his father, a convict in jail. Bob was mortified and couldn't remember ever feeling so hurt. After class he went to Mrs. Prince's office, and the social worker helped validate Bob's feelings. She told Bob that what the teacher had done was very wrong. It was a violation of the teacher's trust to do and say only things that would help students.

She helped Bob understand that sometimes adults make stupid mistakes, sometimes because they have problems of their own.

Mrs. Prince also helped Bob deal with those of his peers who took advantage of the situation to tease and humiliate him. She suggested that Bob pay no attention and not let the other students get satisfaction from being able to upset him. Bob tried it and somehow was able to ignore the comments, and lo and behold, the comments stopped. Usually people who take advantage of such situations do so only because it makes them feel good to make someone else feel bad. When that didn't happen, there was no reason for them to continue the teasing, and it stopped.

Bob suggested that since there were other kids in school whose parents were in jail or had been in jail, perhaps they could all get together and share their experiences so they wouldn't feel so alone. The social worker thought that was an excellent idea and soon started a therapy group. Bob graduated with good grades and has started his first year in college. In some ways, he is stronger now than he was before.

CHAPTER ◊ 9

Why Do I Need Therapy?

You certainly do not have to seek therapy, but there are many reasons why it might be a good idea. You should have enough information to make an informed decision about whether to go.

There are as many misconceptions and stereotypes about therapy as there are about jail and people who wind up in jail. The only way to correct misconceptions and stereotypes is to have accurate information. Let's look at the common errors people make when they think or talk about therapy.

ONLY SICK PEOPLE GO TO THERAPY

Nothing could be further from the truth. In fact, certified therapists go to therapy for many years as part of their training. They do so to learn about themselves and to be as healthy as possible so that they can help others. Therapists know that one can always do better, learn more, develop further, find more happiness, or cope with problems better. Human beings never finish developing and learning. To give yourself the best advantage possible, you might consider therapy as a means toward self-actualization (becoming all that one can become).

People may go to therapy because they are having a problem in their lives that they can't solve on their own. We all have habitual ways of doing things and of viewing the world. We often view things in the way we have been taught to. We internalize (take in or imitate) the viewpoints, values, and ideas of those persons who have been most significant in our lives: parents, friends, relatives, grandparents, teachers, or others who have at one time or another had a special influence on our lives. Often we can see things only the way these people have.

Suppose we were raised alone on a desert island by someone who was blind. That person could teach us many things, but not the differences in colors. To bring the example closer to home, suppose we were raised by parents who believed that it was bad to smile or laugh. We would grow up feeling bad about ourselves whenever we smiled or laughed. We would try hard to deny those feelings and would develop ways of avoiding anything that amused or pleased us. We would grow up feeling that something as natural and human as smiling or laughing was wrong, and we would try to deny this important aspect of our humanity.

Well, things are not always that dramatic or simple, but people do grow up with views and thoughts that are not correct. They may have learned these viewpoints from their parents and may have taught them to us. Therapy can help us to identify those things within ourselves and help us realize that it is not wrong to think or feel certain things that are natural to think or feel. The therapist may suggest alternative ways of viewing the world. The therapist may suggest that not everyone sees things the way our parents do or we do. Once we know that there are alternative viewpoints, we can make decisions for ourselves as to how to proceed with our lives. A good therapist helps to point out all the alternatives to people and helps them to make decisions for themselves.

Personal Loss

Experts know from experience that certain events in a child's life may influence their future life in unhealthy ways. For example, when children lose a parent, especially a mother, at an early age, they often can be depressed or be more vulnerable to depression for the rest of their lives. Often children blame themselves for the death of a parent, because very young children believe that everything that happens around them or to them is the result of something that they have done or even thought. If children have an experienced and caring therapist to work with them at the time they lose their parent, they often suffer less and are not as vulnerable to depression later in life.

The way teenagers feel when a parent is in prison is not much different from their feeling at the death of a parent. Many people recommend that they see a therapist as a preventive measure. A therapist can help the teenager understand and cope with the event so that it will have a less serious influence on his or her later life. We go to the doctor for checkups to make sure we are healthy. Sometimes people forget that the mind is a part of the body, and it also needs to be kept healthy. It too can develop problems without our realizing it. Especially when something as traumatic as a parent's being jailed happens, perhaps we should see a professional who can give our mind a checkup or cure small problems before they become large problems. We get only one head, one mind, and it is our job to take care of it.

People are often afraid of things that have to do with the mind and the way we think, because they do not understand it as well as other parts of the body. Most people aren't afraid of a cold or an earache because they are used to going to the doctor for such ailments. No stigma is attached to catching a cold or having an earache. No one blames them. But because we do not understand the mind as well, people are sometimes afraid of therapy and attach a negative stigma to people who seek help from a therapist. In fact, it is wrong to blame people for any kind of problem that they might be having, but it is certainly *not* wrong to do something about solving problems or preventing problems from starting.

THERAPISTS MAKE YOU TALK ABOUT PRIVATE THINGS

That is usually not true. Therapists and counselors are like any other professionals: There are good ones and not so good ones. Good therapists will not make you talk about anything that you do not want to talk about or are not ready to talk about. They may suggest that something is important to talk about and that it may help you to do so, but the decision is always left up to you. Therapists are not in the business of making people do anything they don't want to do. In fact, it is usually the opposite. They want to make sure that you do only those things you really want to, not simply what someone else wants. Of course, it is the therapists' job to point out things that are not good for you, but they can't control what you do and don't want to.

WHY SHOULD I PAY JUST TO TALK TO SOMEONE?

The reasons for this are many. To begin with, even well-intentioned people who love and care about you are often too involved in your situation to be objective. They may be feeling as frightened and anxious as you are about what has happened. What a therapist tries to do is different from what a friend or relative tries to do. The truth often is that you need both. You need your friends and relatives to talk with and help you, and you may need a therapist to help in ways that they cannot. Friends and relatives can give advice and comfort, protect you, and sometimes listen to you and help you feel understood. Therapists may do some of those things, but often can do other things that you might also need. Therapists help you to think things out for yourself. They help you learn about yourself and the strengths and resources that you may have available. They help you search for the truth with nothing to gain themselves, since they are not usually involved in your life.

For example, you might need to choose whether to go on living with your mother or move to your grandmother's. Your mother may want you to live with her because she is lonely or needs to have you with her. Your grandmother may want you to live with her for the same reasons, or because she believes that your mother may be too overwhelmed with her own worries to provide you everything you need. People you talk to may be on your mother's side because they are closest to her. Others may be on your grandmother's side. Therapists are only on your side. It is their responsibility to have only your best interest in mind. You may need support from someone who is not involved but can help you look at the situation from every angle and decide for yourself what is in your best interest.

WHAT CAN A THERAPIST TELL ME THAT I DON'T ALREADY KNOW?

Qualified therapists have studied and practiced helping people for many years. They learn from the experience of many other therapists who have worked with thousands of people like yourself. They have studied the ways in which we try to avoid the truth about matters because we are afraid or because we feel so overwhelmed at the time that it is hard to think clearly.

Here is an example of a teenager who was recommended to a therapist. James was thirteen, with big brown eyes and short black hair. He was having trouble in school for the first time. The teachers reported that he seemed unable to concentrate and was often found looking out the window, doodling, or otherwise not paying attention. His homework assignments were either late or missing, and he had failed his last three tests. The only subject he seemed to do well in was math.

James was an only child living with his mother and grandmother. His father had been in prison for six months on a twelve-year sentence for manslaughter. James's father had accidentally killed a man during a fight in a bar. James's mother worked long hours as a home attendant, and the family's only other source of income was the grandmother's social security.

James had never been in trouble before. He usually got passing grades and certainly never had any behavior problems. His mother was at her wits' end. It was all she could do to keep things together and to cope with her own isolation and loneliness in her husband's absence. The school social worker recommended that James see a therapist for an evaluation toward possible psychotherapy.

At the first session James had very little to say. He didn't like the idea of being there, and he was determined not to say anything that might cause him to have to return. Nevertheless James and the therapist agreed to meet once a week for two months; then, if he didn't want to continue, they would decide together on some other way to address his problems.

Since James wouldn't talk at first, the therapist began to talk for him. He said he suspected that the reason James wouldn't talk was fear that something he might say would get him in trouble with his mother. She had told him that she didn't want anyone to cry over spilled milk, that his father was in jail and nothing anyone said or did was going to change that. They would all simply have to get on with their lives. The therapist told James that in many ways this was unfair to him. He said talking about it was too painful for his mother and she needed to block it out to be able to keep the family together. But he also said he suspected that James had a lot of thoughts and feelings about his father, and maybe a lot of questions. He said that he worked in a jail and would be glad to answer any questions James might have about what jail was really like. He also offered to make arrangements for James to talk to his father on the phone.

James's face lighted up, but he tried to hide it. The therapist emphasized that whatever they spoke about was confidential, that no one, not even his mother, would know about it.

Eventually, in the fourth session, James began to ask

about jail. He had dozens of questions. He wanted to know how people lived in jail. Was it true that people got beaten up, or that men sometimes got raped? He wanted to know about the jail that his father was in. After all this, James admitted that in fact he felt terrible. He worried constantly about his father, and wondered if he would ever see him again. He had nightmares about his father in jail. Some nights he even had nightmares about himself in jail. People used to tell him that he was just like his father; did that mean that he would someday go to jail also?

Soon the two months were up. James seemed to forget about the earlier agreement, and he never asked if he could go somewhere else or do something else. He seemed to enjoy the sessions. In addition, he began to do better in school. All James had really needed was someone who would answer his questions and listen to anything he needed to talk about. Once he was able to talk freely, he didn't need to daydream about these fears in school.

James learned that what he was thinking and feeling was normal, that even though his mother chose not to talk about these things, it was okay for him to do so. He learned that what works best for one person may not work so well for another. He learned that he was entitled to his own thoughts, feelings, and questions. He discovered that these thoughts stay with you despite all efforts to block them out. In fact, the thoughts persisted in his day and night dreams until he was able to talk about them freely.

James also learned that words are very powerful things. They are often the only way we have of making sense of something that has happened. Once he was allowed to use whatever words he wanted, he was able to make connections between what he was thinking and what was happening to him. He was able to formulate and test out new ideas. Most important, because he was able to use words to express what he was thinking and feeling, he was able to understand things and himself better.

Once you understand something, you can make changes. James understood that he had choices. He had a choice to communicate with his father on the phone and by writing. He also had a choice to be like his father in some ways and not in other ways. He could choose, for example, to play football like his father, but not to drink the way his father did. He learned that his father had made choices in his life and that was okay, but that James had to make his own choices. James learned that he had some control over how things would turn out for himself; he learned that things do not happen by chance or by coincidence, but usually as a result of the choices that we make. Of course, he did not choose to have a father who drank or who was in prison, but even so, he could choose how to cope with the fact. He also learned that he had had nothing to do with what happened to his father, that there was nothing he could have done to prevent it, and there was nothing he could do about what happened to his father in the future.

James was lucky. His school had observed that he was having a reaction to his father's imprisonment, and they tried to get help for him. He was also lucky because his mother agreed. James is likely to do just fine with his life. He has learned things about himself that he will always be able to use. James is not likely to see the inside of a jail because he has learned a very important lesson. He has learned that to ask for help made him stronger, not weaker. Everyone has problems; if we didn't have problems, we wouldn't be human. The difference is that some people choose to do something about them, and others are afraid or have no opportunity to seek assistance.

CHAPTER ◊ 10

How to Ask for Help

Most of this book has been about coping when a parent is incarcerated, whether temporarily in jail, or for an extended time in prison. This is important because having information can be essential when dealing with any crisis. In part, that is because crisis leads to having to make decisions, choices, and changes. However, information alone is not enough when there are important choices to be made. It is only the beginning. Because of the nature of crisis, we can become overwhelmed, confused, frightened, anxious, and even depressed. All of a sudden nothing seems familiar. Long-thought-of plans and assumptions no longer apply. Things change.

Change, especially sudden change, can be frightening. Because of this we may need help from someone who is not involved in the confusion, someone who can help us to think clearly and consider alternatives that we may not have seen. Besides, in a crisis, simply talking is crucial.

That is how human beings cope with and recover from crises. When someone dies or we are faced with a tragedy, we need to talk about it over and over again with as many people as possible. Talking helps us to put things in a new and different perspective.

MOURNING

Often tragedy involves loss. When a parent is incarcerated, many losses or potential losses may be involved—the loss of that parent, of the way things were, of the way that we imagined they were going to be. It can represent loss of security and of self-esteem. It can mean the loss of a home, friends, or other important things. It often involves the loss of the family's financial security.

All loss requires mourning, the process by which we feel and express grief. Mourning of necessity involves sharing and talking. When people lose a loved one, they tend to talk about the person often. That is the only way they can successfully separate from the person enough to be able to go on with their lives. Mourning often involves losses other than people. When we lose someone or something that is important to us, our mind attempts to mourn (or separate from) that which was lost. Sometimes people say that you shouldn't keep talking about something sad, or that you shouldn't look back. Have you ever heard the expression, "Enough already, move on." That is wrong. People should be allowed to talk about something they have lost for as long as they need to. Only then will they be able to move on.

When a parent goes to jail, it involves changes for the whole family. Everyone is in some way affected. Counselors who work with families understand this very well. They have seen entire families change as a result of something that has changed with one member. Such counselors can help to spot problems before they get too bad. In addition, they are used to finding ways to improve problems that have already gotten bad.

THE FIRST STEP TO HELP

The first thing that you might have to overcome in seeking help is the stereotype about professional help. Stereotypes come from ignorance; they are usually incorrect and rarely helpful. It is very important for you to do what will be helpful to you, despite what anyone else may say. What you choose to do will affect your life much more than those people who are commenting on your choices.

Many people around you would be glad to offer you suggestions and assistance in getting help. For example, try talking to a teacher, a school counselor, the principal, or even the gym coach. There is also your church, the parish priest, minister, or rabbi. There are neighbors, relatives, and grandparents, and of course you may have another parent at home. There may be an older brother or sister who could put you in touch with help. There is probably a toll-free number for social services or child protective services in your area. Clinics and social service agencies are listed in the phone book. Many hospitals have outpatient clinics where you might be able to walk in and ask for help. Children's hospitals often have excellent outpatient clinics where counselors and therapists are ready to help people from the neighborhood.

You may have to approach your other parent: your mother, if it is your father who has been incarcerated; or your father, if your mother was the one arrested. If your grandmother or a relative is taking care of you, you might have to ask her to get you help. You could simply say that you are upset by what has happened and you would like to speak with a counselor.

You might be upset about what is happening to another member of your family and want to get help for that person. It is often easier to ask for help than suggest to someone else that they need help. People can often see the problem in someone else much more easily than they can within themselves.

If you are having trouble doing this or just can't bring yourself to say the words, you might ask a parent to read this book with you, or show him or her this chapter and ask for an opinion.

If you feel unable to approach you own family, you may need another adult to help you. That is when it might be easier to talk to a teacher, a neighbor, or someone you feel comfortable with. The important thing is to keep trying. It is important for your life that you get the help you need. It is important in helping you with your current problems and in preventing future problems. There is nothing wrong with asking for help when you need it. There *is* something wrong with ignoring your own needs and pretending that everything is okay.

FACTS ABOUT COUNSELING

If you plan to see a counselor, it is important to know certain things about counseling. First of all, you have a right to speak with someone that you are comfortable with. Of course, you might not feel completely comfortable the first few times you talk to someone new, but within a relatively short time you should begin to feel a good relationship with the counselor.

People have tried counseling, and because they were never able to establish rapport with one counselor, have decided that counseling doesn't work. It may not be the counseling that doesn't work, just the counselor. Or a particular counselor may work well with most people but not with you. You have a right as the patient, or client, to ask for a change until you find someone that you feel comfortable with.

Above all, if you feel uncomfortable with a counselor you should try to tell the counselor so. He or she may not be aware of your reaction and may be able to help you understand why you feel uncomfortable. Ultimately, the counselor may be able to direct you to someone better for you. If you can't approach the counselor, try talking to the person in charge of the place where you are receiving the help. If it is a private therapist, try another therapist. You might ask others who are in therapy or who know something about counseling to recommend someone.

TYPES OF THERAPY

There are many schools of therapy and many, many different types of counselors. Counselors often specialize. Some work with adults, some with children or adolescents. Some counselors or therapists specialize in working with families or couples. Some are experts on crisis intervention. Others have special training in long-term psychotherapy designed to bring about personality changes. Many have experience with several types of treatment and can combine techniques depending on your needs.

Therapists and counselors have different types of training. Many professionals are licensed in certain states. For example, psychiatric social workers, psychologists, psychiatrists, pastoral counselors, and some psychiatric nurses are licensed to practice counseling in New York. In addition many professionals take additional training after they receive their license to practice.

This is important to know, because many people practice as counselors who are not trained or certified to do so. Anyone can call himself a psychotherapist, but no one can use any of the professional titles above without a license to do so. In addition, no one can practice as a psychoanalyst without certification.

Of course, having a license doesn't mean that a person would be good for you, but at least you know that he or she is qualified to help. Then the question arises whether a particular approach or personality works well with you and your problems. After a relatively short time, you should begin to feel that the person listens to you and understands you.

For some people, individual therapy or counseling works best; for others, family therapy or group therapy. Sometimes different types of therapy can be combined. It is not unusual for someone to be in both individual and group therapy at the same time.

In the final analysis, it is important to know that help is available. Growing up is not easy. Most people have a difficult time with it. It is hard enough to grow up when you face no drastic changes. Even if everything goes well, simply managing the different stages in life can be difficult. Childhood, adolescence, adulthood all have their unique challenges. Beginning school, moving, first dates, and making friends all require new coping skills. When something happens like losing a parent or having a parent imprisoned, it can stress you past the point where you can cope on your own. Ask for help when you need it.

Appendix

RESOURCES

It is estimated that there are approximately 1,500,000 children of incarcerated parents in the United States. As the child of an incarcerated parent, you may be experiencing several problems that are common to other children in your situation.

When your parent was arrested or incarcerated, you experienced a trauma. Such trauma often results in changes in the way you feel or behave. You might feel increased anger or aggressiveness, nervousness or anxiety, or difficulty concentrating in school or finishing a book. At times you may feel guilt that you are okay while your parent is in jail. This is called survivors guilt. Many suggestions have been made throughout this book as to how to go about seeking help. A few of them are reviewed here, with other alternatives you can try to get the support you need.

1. Try talking with your other parent if another parent is at home, and explain that you need help.
2. Try talking with other adults:
   A teacher, principal, counselor, or social worker at your school.
   A person at your church or temple such as a priest, sister, minister, or rabbi.
   A trusted neighbor or friend's parents.
   A counselor at any youth organization such as the YMCA.

3. Using the phone book, call a number listed under Counseling, Youth or Family Services, Department of Social Services, or Special Social Services for Children.

Places to call or write for information

Prison Fellowship
Post Office Box 17500
Washington, DC 20041-0500
703/478-0100

> Has listings of referrals across the country. Also publishes *Inside Journal*, a newspaper written by inmates for inmates.

National Institute of Corrections
1960 Industrial Circle
Longmont, CO 80501
303/682-0213

> Publishes *Directory of Programs Serving Families of Adult Offenders*

Pacific Oaks College and Children's Programs
The Center for Children of Incarcerated Parents
714 West California Boulevard
Pasadena, CA 91105
818/397-1300

American Correctional Association
8025 Laurel Lakes Court
Laurel MD 20707
301/206-5100

The Fortune Society
39 West 19th Street
New York, NY 10011
212/206-7070
> Publishes *Fortune News*

Glossary

bail Money or property deposited by an inmate as a promise to return for court appointments.
bench warrant Warrant issued by a judge when a defendant fails to keep a court appointment.
block or cell block Housing area with individual cells.
bond Bail bond representing part (usually 10 percent) of the total bail.
bondsman Person who makes a business of issuing bail bonds for defendants, for a fee.
classification Committee that interviews new detainees to determine where they should be housed based on psychological, emotional, and other factors.
commissary "Store" where inmates may purchase candy, cigarettes, toiletries, and other items, using their own funds being kept in the Cashiers Office.
contraband Items not permitted in the possession of inmates, ranging from cash money to home-made weapons.
detainee An incarcerated person; a defendant; an inmate whose charges have not yet been adjudicated.
detox Slang for detoxification, the process by which a person's body is made free of drugs.
felon Person convicted of a felony, the most serious category of crime.
gang Group of inmates assigned to the same prison work, such as the Paint Gang.
good time Ten days per month reduction of sentence for inmates who abide by the rules and standards of conduct.

infraction Violation of acceptable standards of conduct.

parole Conditional release from incarceration. The parolee is subject to certain rules, violation of which results in return to prison to serve the remainder of the sentence.

predicate felon Inmate with a prior felony conviction, who is liable to a longer sentence for the same crime.

probation "Suspended sentence." The person is permitted to remain free during the term of the sentence providing no further arrests or convictions occur. If convicted on a second charge before completion of probation, the suspended sentence is added to the new sentence.

violation Failure to obey the conditions of parole or probation, usually leading to a return to jail.

For Further Reading

Base, D. *As Free as an Eagle: The Inmates Family Survival Guide*. American Correctional Association, 1991.

Martin, D., and Sussman, P. *Committing Journalism: The Prison Writings of Red Hog*. New York: W.W. Norton & Company, 1993.

Morris, P. *Prisoners and Their Families*. New York: Holt Publishing Company, 1965.

Sachs, Albie. *The Jail Diary of Albie Sachs*. New York: McGraw-Hill, 1967.

Vonnegut, Kurt. *Jailbird*: New York: Delacorte Press/Seymour Lawrence, 1979.

The following books can be ordered from the addresses given:

Last Train to Alcatraz, The Autobiography of Leon (Whitey) Thompson; and *The Merry-Go-Round* (sequel to *Last Train to Alcatraz*), Winter Book Publisher, P.O. Box 219, Fiddletown, CA 95629.

All Kinds of Families, by Norma Simon, A. Whitman, Albert and Company, Niles, Il 60648.

Joey's Visit, by Donna Jones, Family Matters, c/o Cooperative Extension, 1050 West Genesse Street, Syracuse, NY 13204 (1.50 plus $.50 postage).

My Mother and I Are Going Strong (in both English and Spanish), New Seed Press, 1665 Euclid Ave., Berkeley, CA 94709 (3.50 plus $1 postage).

When Can Daddy Come Home? Martha Whitmore Hichman, Abingdon Press, Nashville, TN 37202.

A Visit to the Big House, Oliver Butterworth (includes Spanish translation), Evelyn Herrmann-Keeling Families in Crisis, Inc. 30 Arbor Street Hartford, CT 06106.

I Know How You Feel, Because This Happened to Me: A Handbook for Kids with a Parent in Prison, Louise Rosenkrantz, M.Ed., Prison MATCH, 2121 Russell Street, Berkeley, CA 94705.

Index

A
abortion, 65–66
acquittal, 55
adjournment, 5, 50, 52
Alcoholics Anonymous, 75–76
appeals, 53–54, 68
arraignment, 5, 7
arrest, 6
   drug, 64

B
bail, 11
   bond, 7
   forfeiting, 7
   system, unfair, 4
blame, self, 88–89, 97
bonding, 42
book and case number, 15, 35

C
Cauchon, Dennis, 64
cell, 8, 19–20
   block, 15
change
   in family roles, 90–91, 105–106
   fear of, 104–105
   opportunity for, 17
   from prison to freedom, 73–74
child abuse, 66, 81
choices, making, 85, 89, 103
clinic, medical, 9, 14, 15, 61
clothing, inmates', 25
commissary, 9, 19, 24
community service, 7, 63
confidentiality, in therapy, 44, 81
conflict
   family, 80
   of jail groups, 20
consequences, living with, 31–32
contempt of court, 66
contraband, 24, 26, 28
conviction
   beyond reasonable doubt, 5, 54
   of innocent person, 53–54
corrections officers, 8, 11, 18, 20–21, 24, 69
counseling, 14, 43–44, 107–108
   family, 76–78, 81–82, 109
   jail, 15
   prison, 61, 68, 79
counselor, 43, 56, 66, 70

jail, 9, 27
prison, 75–76
rapport with, 107–108
crime
   nonviolent, 66–67
   violent, 73
   white-collar, 67
culture, prison, 38–39, 67, 70

D
death penalty, 64
debtors' prison, 62
defendant, 5, 7, 51, 52, 53
defense attorney, 51, 52, 55
depression
   family's, 78, 97
   inmate's, 27
deterrent, prison term as, 63–65
district attorney, 5, 51
dormitory, 8, 15, 19–20
drugs
   abuse of, 3, 16–17, 22–23, 40–42, 44–45, 75, 87
   deprivation of, 16
   smuggling of, 26
   war on, 4–5, 40, 63
drug treatment program, 14

E
electronic surveillance, 3–4
embarrassment
   of having parent in jail, 32
   of parent in jail, 33, 74, 80
evidence, 11
   insufficient, 5, 7, 56
   probable cause, 6
examination
   Article 730, 52

physical, 9, 15–16

F
father
   in jail, 2–3, 10–12, 13–23, 28–29, 32–36
   in prison, 70–71, 74–79, 91–94, 100–103
fear
   of imprisonment, 63–64
   in jail life, 15, 21
feelings, 87–88
   entitlement to, 31–32, 43, 102–103
   expressing, 26
   to parent in jail, 34–36
felony, 6, 63
fights
   jail, 20–21, 26–27, 39
   prison, 69
fine, 6, 7, 63
freedom, adjustment to, 73–74

G
Gottfredson, Mark, 64
grand jury, 6
guilt feelings
   children's, 31, 87–88
   about thoughts, 2–3, 46–48, 77–78
guilt, reasonable doubt of, 55
guilty
   finding of, 5
   plea of, 7, 51, 56–57

H
hearing, court, 5, 50–60
help, asking for, 43–44, 80–82, 103, 104–109

INDEX

house (jail), 8, 15, 35

I
incarceration, 8, 13, 63, 105
inmate, 8
   advantage taken by, 18
   visits to, 9–10
innocence, presumption of, 5

J
jail
   life in, 8–10, 13–23
   pending trial, 7
   vs. prison, 14–15, 67–70
   sentence for misdemeanor, 6
judge, 7, 52, 53–54, 56–57
jury, 54–55
justice, system of, 3–4, 65–66

L
laws, criminal, 6–7
learning, ways of, 84–85
legal insanity, 52–53
Lehman, Joseph, 64

M
mail, inmates', 10, 15
maximum-security prison, 61
mental illness, 9, 15
minimum-security prison, 61
misdemeanor, 6, 63
money, inmates', 9, 19, 24
mother, in jail, 41–49
mourning, 105–106

N
Narcotics Anonymous, 48

O
overcrowding, prison, 63, 73

P
pardon, 68
parentified child, 45–46
parole, 52, 70, 72–82
   cutbacks in, 4
   violation of, 80
Parole Board, 51, 67, 71, 72, 74, 78
perjury, 66
plea
   guilty or not guilty, 7
   not guilty, 54
plea bargaining, 51–52, 56–57
postponement, hearing, 5
predicate, 70–71, 75
prejudice, 65, 67, 85
   in jail, 14–15
pressure, jail, 21, 36
prison, 61–71
   vs. jail, 14–15, 67–70
   population growth, 3, 4, 39–40, 62–64
   sentence for felony, 6
probation, 7, 52, 57, 72–73
programs
   jail, 14, 39–40
   prison, 75
property, theft of, 11, 25
prosecutor, 51, 52, 54–55, 56–57
protection
   of jail inmates, 15–16, 18–20
   in prison "family," 39, 69
pseudofamilies, female, 39
psychiatrist, 52
publicity, coping with, 58–60

punishment, 63, 68–69
   as deterrent to crime, 62
   harshness of, 62, 63–64

R
rape, 10–11
   in jail, 13, 39
   in prison, 102
recognizance, release on own, 7
rehabilitation services, 14, 61–62, 68
relationships
   heterosexual, 38, 66
   homosexual, 39
   marital, 76–77
   mother-daughter, 48–49
   prison, 69–70
   with self, 83–91
release
   date, 68
   early ("good time"), 69, 73
Rikers Island, 4
rules
   parole, 72, 79–80
   visiting, 24–25, 26, 36–37

S
schools, prison, 14, 61, 68
search
   of inmates, 15, 27–28
   of visitors, 24
secrecy, code of, 18, 69–70
security procedures, 27–28, 36
self-esteem, 86–87, 89–90
   loss of, 32, 74, 84, 109
sentence
   for felony, 63, 67–68
   indeterminate, 72–82
   for misdemeanor, 63

prison, 5–6, 51, 54–55
   tendency to longer, 4
   time served included in, 51
sex, laws about, 66
social worker, 43, 44–49, 92–94
solitary confinement, 69
stereotypes
   coping with, 59
   about therapy, 95–103, 106
   of women in jail, 40–41
suicide
   tendency toward, 69, 81
   thoughts of, 15–16, 27
Sykes, Gresham, 38

T
talk, need to, 43, 99–100, 105
telephone, use in jail, 10, 15
therapist, 43, 44, 56, 95–103
   family, 77
   rapport with, 109
therapy
   reasons for, 95–103
   types of, 108–109
trial, 54–55
   children attending, 55–56
   preparing for, 11–12, 51–52
   waiving right to, 7, 51, 57

U
uncertainty, painfulness of, 5–6, 57, 58

V
violence
   in jail, 8, 11, 39
   in prison, 70
visits
   conjugal, 20

INDEX

daughter's refusal of, 28–29
inmate's refusal of, 27, 32–36
jail, 9–10, 13, 17, 24–37

W
women in jail, 38–49

work programs, 9, 61–62, 68
work release, 61
worry
   family's, about jailed parent, 2–3, 9, 13, 16, 27, 58, 81, 87, 102
   woman inmate's, 40

MARION JUNIOR HIGH LIBRARY
Two Patriot Drive
Marion, AR 72364